Janice Elliott

Janice Elliott was born in Derbyshire and brought up in wartime Nottingham, the setting for her best-seller SECRET PLACES which won a Southern Arts award and was also made into a prize-winning film. She read English at St Anne's College, Oxford, left a career in journalism for full-time writing and now has twenty-three novels to her credit as well as a volume of short stories, THE NOISE FROM THE ZOO, and five children's books. Consistently acclaimed by the critics, she has been described as 'one of the best novelists writing in England'.

Janice Elliott and her husband now live in Cornwall which inspired her novel THE SADNESS OF WITCHES. For many years she was a fiction reviewer for the *Sunday Telegraph*. She is a fellow of the Royal Society of Literature.

SCEPTRE

Also by Janice Elliott

Cave with Echoes
The Somnambulists
The Godmother
The Buttercup Chain
The Singing Head
Angels Falling
The Kindling

England Trilogy

A State of Peace
Private Life
Heaven on Earth

A Loving Eye
The Honey Tree
Summer People
Secret Places
The Country of her Dreams
Magic
The Italian Lesson
Dr Gruber's Daughter
The Sadness of Witches
Life on the Nile
Necessary Rites
The Noise From the Zoo
City of Gates

For Children

The Birthday Unicorn
Alexander in the Land of Mog
The Incompetent Dragon
The King Awakes
The Empty Throne

Figures in the Sand

JANICE ELLIOTT

SCEPTRE

First published in 1994 by Hodder and Stoughton
A division of Hodder Headline PLC
A Sceptre Book 1995

10 9 8 7 6 5 4 3 2 1

All characters in this publication are fictitious and any resemblance to real persons, living or dead, is purely coincidental.

British Library Cataloguing in Publication Data

Elliott, Janice
Figures in the Sand
I. Title
823.914 [F]

ISBN 0 340 64693 4

Printed and bound in Great Britain by
Cox and Wyman Ltd, Reading, Berkshire

Hodder and Stoughton
A division of Hodder Headline PLC
338 Euston Road
London NW1 3BH

Why do we aim so highly, so bravely,
so briefly? Why hanker for countries scorched
by an alien sun? What exile from home
        can avoid himself?

Horace, *Odes*, Book II, 16

1

The two bodies, the girl and her child, were found a couple of miles from the city. Her eyes, that had been open, were stopped with sand. She had torn at her bright red skirt to wrap the child. It lay curled at her breast as if it might still suckle life from her, even though she was dead.

2

What am I doing here? That's what I want to know.

My name is Otto. I am of medium height with brownish hair and a reasonably cheerful nature.

My master says I make him laugh and I know he feels low sometimes, missing the lady Livia. We hope she might come to join us, although the journey would be dangerous.

But I must tell you where we are. A forsaken place but apparently a strategic one. It was once called Tadmor. My master is a bit of a historian so he has gone back to the old name.

History means nothing to me. As far as I am concerned this is a ruined city between desert and mountains, infernally hot in summer and ball-freezing in winter.

In the way of the new Romans my master was given the name of Octavius and when he was sent to set up the garrison in Tadmor, the title of General. He says the first Romans sacked it once. Maybe that's why it's just a heap of old ruins, as far as I can see.

This is the longest posting I've had – I can't tell you how long because I've stopped counting. The General says we're going to be relieved but no one comes. Maybe they've forgotten us.

I tell you, I can put up with the stinking climate and the scorpions. I'm a soldier so I don't worry my head much about why we're here. But there is one relief I can't wait much longer for. Myself, I don't fancy the arrangements some of the men have come to – the sort of stuff soldiers are pushed to if they're without women as long as we've been. What I've had my eye on for months now is a girl I saw beating fleeces by the stream. She comes every so often with the other women from the black tents. She wears a red dress with scarves and bangles and a length of cloth or thin stuff edged with gold coins that's meant to cover her hair. I don't know what language they're talking, the lieutenant says it's the Bedouin dialect but when the women are together they shout a lot and laugh and sometimes they'll sing. They've got rough tempers, you can tell.

Not to give offence, I've got to admit that the first thing I noticed about her was her haunches. She bent to dip her fleece with her legs straight so you couldn't miss what a fine pair they were. Strong, well-rounded, useful haunches. Then one of the others laughed and yelled at her and she looked up and saw me watching. I couldn't tell if she was angry. I don't think so. She didn't shriek or run away. She just snatched her veil across her face.

I like it when she rests her back and stands with her hands on her hips stretching her spine.

Of course, it would be an offence. The Bedouin are supposed to be a touchy lot. If her father or brother or husband for all I know, didn't slit my throat first, I'd be up on a charge pronto.

Minimum penalty, loss of pay and three weeks' solitary in the cage. Maximum, crucifixion.

All the same, I can't help thinking, if I caught her alone. There's talk that they're bringing some whores in soon. I'll believe that when I see it.

It's plain to me what we all need. Action. That's what we were trained for. I'm not bloodthirsty, I'm a professional, it's that simple. But all we get is patrols and the odd skirmish.

We don't even know who the enemy is.

Now and then, in the distance where the desert stretches to the Euphrates, Octavius imagines he can see figures, fore-runners perhaps of an army. Then he finds he has a mote of sand in his eye, they are pictures conjured by his distorted vision, temporary flaws on his retina.

In the dry season he lives and sleeps in a tent in the Temple of Bel. At this outpost at the end of history he has learned not to count the passing of days, nor to dwell on the unreason of his mission.

If he were to turn now and look, he might find melancholy so close behind him he would smell its dark breath. Instead, the General consults his books, writes his journal, maps this amazing territory, and just before dusk – when thoughts of Livia most pain him, when he remembers the swell of her belly, her steady consenting welcome, the scent of her fingers snapping off a sprig of rosemary on their evening stroll in the garden – then General Octavius pulls on his rough Arab cloak and walks away from the encampment with its flickering fires and smell of goat or mutton cooking.

On these evenings Octavius finds a consolation he cannot explain to himself in the Valley of Tombs, among the towers of the dead.

The child he has never seen was born long ago, of course. A girl, named Paulina. Livia and Octavius had made secret plans just before he left.

On their last evening walk in the garden they had said little about the posting to Syria, or the fact that the wives and families – even of officers – were not to accompany the Legion.

Livia had said: 'Maybe it means you won't be gone long.'

Her tone was wistful. She had known she was marrying a soldier and how their lives would be, and over sixteen years she had put up with the constant upheavals. Rufus had been born in Aswan and grown up in a succession of temporary quarters. The nomad life appeared to have done him no harm. A good-looking boy of medium intelligence and great sweetness of nature, he had been company for Livia and an easy mixer who made new friends, got into normal scrapes and seemed to accept his father's absences without resentment.

All the same, Livia and Octavius had been thankful when in Rufus's thirteenth year, Octavius had been recalled to headquarters at Tivoli and a more or less honorary desk-job as Commander of the Praetorian Guard.

Not that Octavius relished the appointment. At forty-five he felt ten years younger, not ready for retirement, impatient with politics and inaction. Still, there had always been a reflective side to his nature. Now he would have time to indulge it. He wondered about history, if there were anything to be learned, for instance, from those other Romans, the first. He strolled in the ruins of Hadrian's Villa and pondered the nature of decline. Did all civilisations at some point grow weary? As in the ageing of a man, did powerful cultures leave the great stage, take to their armchairs and at last to their beds, prefiguring their graves? The dead emperor in his mausoleum might listen with a kind of compliance for the barbarian shout. And then it would all happen again. First, the savage would piss on the throne he would next occupy in pomp until he, too, fell into folly and decline.

But at this point in his career – what should have been the comfortable evening – Octavius's vigour, the strong pumping of his blood, argued with any serious attempt at philosophy. He rode horseback. He walked miles but could not exhaust himself. He was demanding in bed and Livia was initially startled and then responsive. Ecstatically. Inventively. They were astonished, never glutted, ravenous, in their discovery of middle-aged lust.

So, preoccupied, the two with their appetites, Livia with furnishing her first true home and making her garden – fountains, roses, lavender – were in all innocence shocked and bewildered when Rufus began to get into troubles that could not be dismissed as scrapes. It was as though they had woken up one day and found that the boy had been wickedly bewitched overnight. He was sullen. He was brought home drunk. He said Tivoli was boring, suburban. He refused to take a place at the Academy.

Octavius did not know how to talk to this stranger, his son. He blamed himself. Rufus was sent to a farm in Tuscany. He shrugged off his sentence.

Rufus is now grown, a young man. A lot has happened. Octavius knows this. Yet he still sees his son as he was at their last meeting, the day Rufus went to the farm, when he turned away from his father's clumsy attempt at an embrace, at reconciliation. They never had touched very much. For that, and many other gestures not made, words unspoken, Octavius blames himself. The day Rufus went to the farm, after he had left, Octavius heard Livia's crying, a dry, racked sound, a woman's pain. He tried the door but she had locked it.

Soon after, she told him she was pregnant, four months gone already. The fruit of their ripe love. How proud they were. What a miracle. He kissed her belly, she took his head between her hands, cradled him. They lay in the tangle of sheets, conspirators in a wonderful secret. There was a dish of September figs on the marble floor by the bed, veined and full. The juice spurted.

The orders to Syria arrived the next day, along with the promotion.

That last night in Livia's garden with its view over the hills that tumbled down to Rome, strolling arm-in-arm in the mothy dusk, they spoke as they could not in the house. Indoors there might well be listeners. Even Generals had listeners. Especially Generals.

'But if you're not here,' Livia said.

'Then you must forget about it. It's too dangerous.'

'No. I wanted it for Rufus and we couldn't. Well, you were away and I was young and it didn't seem to matter so much. This is our second chance. The last one. I want this child baptised.' Livia bent to snap off a dead geranium head. There had always been something in her nature you could call valiant or stubborn. She went on firmly and quickly before Octavius could interrupt. 'I know how and where. A secret chapel. A priest. Someone who'll help. Better you don't know any details. Just in case.'

They rested on the stone seat by the cypress. Here Livia had made a pool. There was a golden flick of small fish.

Livia was planning to break the law but her tone was light.

'We must have a code, to tell you it's done. I know. Virgil. Any reference to Virgil. They'd never suspect that.'

She was right. Reading of the ancients was encouraged among the officers and servants of the empire, compulsory at the Academy.

'But you'll be back by then.'

'I expect so.'

Livia shivered.

'The nights are getting colder. Come to bed.'

For once, after loving, Octavius could not sleep. He pulled on his robe and paced the villa and the garden. He paused for a chat with the guard but it was a new man, clearly alarmed at being addressed by the General. He wore the colours not of the Praetorian Guard but the Legion.

'So what do you think of this expedition?' Octavius asked.

'Sir. I don't think. I mean, about politics. But I'll be glad to be away.'

'You don't care for Tivoli?'

'I like action, sir. It's natural, isn't it?'

Octavius nodded. He realised why he could not sleep, what he could not confess to Livia. He too wanted action and his motives were no nobler than those of the common soldier. Campaigns had made of him a fighting animal who could not settle for long by the hearth. His eyes were full of deserts and alien skies. His flesh asked to be tested. It had the habit of endurance. This would be his last chance to try it as you might push a horse to its limit; and the horse rejoiced with you, or seemed to, its heart pumping just this side of bursting; and even after it had been rubbed down and watered and fed, its flanks still shivered, you could see its plumes of breath along with your own in the cold night air beside a fire and a bivouac.

Somewhere forgotten he had read: *and the horse laughed*.

It was nearly dawn. Octavius was ageing, he knew that. But he wanted to go just once more to a dangerous frontier. Then, when that was done, he would like to feel that in company with himself, the territories of the empire and those beyond, would grow out of this age of man into a new nature. The old Roman age of gold. Empires put away, frontiers dissolved, soldiers happy to cultivate their fields, gone home for good.

Did all men share the same wish? That history might keep pace with their own small lives? It never did.

All the same, it was a beguiling illusion to comfort oneself at dawn: to imagine that if he survived this campaign, it would be the last ever fought.

What a change in nature that would be, as astounding as the alteration that took place the day chaos gave birth to form.

Meanwhile the sun had spent the night in India and was now rising in Latium. Octavius heard Livia call and at the same moment the bugle sounded reveille in the barracks of the Second Legion, named for Vespasian.

Octavius slapped his upper arms for warmth and looked south. In Asia the sun would already be up.

Paulina was born in February but it was March before Octavius had Livia's letter. A girl, perfect. Born with long legs.

'So she'll be tall! My side of the family, mother insists – as if inches made her lucky.

'I got the pains just after dinner and she arrived by breakfast-time. Mother fussing. You'd think no child had ever been born before. You are not to worry, my darling. This Syrian business must be settled soon and then you can see our beautiful Paulina.

'I miss you and I wish the mail from Asia were quicker. No one will tell me why there has been nothing since December.

'I've been getting books together for you, since you asked. To encourage you to come home and enjoy the orchard, here are the *Georgics* – all about husbandry. Isn't that a good word?'

All these years later the General reads Virgil's early words. They hold more meaning for him now than they did when he first flicked through that song of praise to the cultivation of nature.

Then, they were a coded signal from Livia that Paulina had been given a Christian baptism. Lately, Octavius finds other more fearful messages.

Countryfolk made homeless, and their scythes
Beaten to straight swords on the blowing forge.
War from the Euphrates to Germany,
Ruptured engagements, violence of nations,
Impious Mars raging the whole world over.

Octavius shuts the book. Perhaps you find what you are looking for, he is feeding his own mood. There are as many consolations as there are warnings in the study of antiquity. Two years after these sombre lines, Octavian was named with justice Augustus, the blessed one, the peacemaker. For the moment, tyrants left the stage.

Odysseus came back to Ithaca to faithful Penelope. Livia said, when she and her friends were silly girls they told their fortunes from Homer. When it came to her turn, she closed her eyes and let the *Odyssey* fall open where it would. And there was Penelope by her hearth in her chair of ivory and silver. Not knowing her husband yet, disguised as he was in rags, but giving him a place by her fire.

And the beggar at her hearth was her husband.

'As though she wouldn't know her own husband,' Livia had said.

Octavius smiles. He hears Livia's voice. At least, she could read Greek. He'd never fully mastered it at college or at the

Academy. His instructor there had been on the non-military staff, Pausonias, a skinny old Greek from Macedonia, with a sharp tongue.

'They tell me you'll go far,' he had said one hot afternoon with thunder brewing. Pausonias refused to open a window because he detested the sound of drilling cadets or anything else martial. 'But it won't be in Greek.' A fat bee was sizzing against the window. Like Octavius, it wanted to get out. For once, he was grateful for the loose tunica, the old dress that the new Romans had arbitrarily adopted.

Octavius had thought himself dismissed and was standing already when Pausonias slapped the text-book shut.

'What's wrong with you, Fidus Octavius? You're intelligent. I've seen you thinking. Or dreaming. Whatever it is you do. You're not one of those foot-stamping savages out there.' Pausonias snorted. He had a narrow, yellow face, the waxy skin of old age, but his eyes were bright with exasperation. 'As though one Roman empire wasn't enough. What kind of life do you want?'

Octavius shifted from one foot to the other. He felt heavy, hot and foolish. There was something about his instructor he had always liked. An odd respect approaching affection.

'Army, sir. A soldier. That's why I'm at the Academy.'

'And what qualities would you say are to be desired in a soldier?'

'Courage, sir? A quick mind? Stamina?'

'You could say the same of a jackal. What a soldier needs as a defender of the city, if he is not to turn and rend the city itself, is the character of a well-bred dog. By nature philosophical and fond of learning, so that he may distinguish between friend and enemy. And can you tell me, boy, who said that?'

'No, sir.'

'Plato. He thought a lot of dogs. He also said that in the breeding of this noble dog-soldier, literature must come before gymnastics.'

Young Octavius was sweating. He wondered how Pausonias could breathe in this temperature. He was meeting friends to swim in the pool by the ruined temple. A spring fed it, no one knew its depth, he was thirsty for the bottomless green. If you dived too deep and the cold cramped you, you could drown. Screened by the ilex grove and the temple, there was another pool for the women, daughters and wives of the Academy, the Legion and the Guard, forbidden to the men. The boys of the Academy dared each other to spy. Last week Octavius had caught a glimpse of a girl, one among others, laughing. They were towelling themselves dry. Only she did not look over her shoulder to see if the boys were watching.

He heard Pausonias sigh, and blinked.

'Your problem, Fidus Octavius, is that you are a young and healthy animal, utterly confused by nature's inconsiderate surge. You'd better go.'

'Sir?'

'But you'll remember one day. If you live that long the time will come when you'll think of Plato's dog. I fear you will never learn much Greek but you have it in you to be alone with the difficult questions.'

Pausonias waved his hand, a dismissive, slicing gesture.

'Now go away and swim, which is all you have in mind. Go away. And don't salute me.'

Octavius left Pausonias with the weary bee still stunning itself against the pane, in the small room, counting his amber worry-beads.

He met Livia for the first time that afternoon.

When he came back to Tivoli that autumn, from summer manoeuvres, Octavius heard that Pausonias had died. The Academy was by no means sorry to see the end of the Greek. There had been complaints from parents that he was a subversive influence. He put ideas into a few heads. He drank too much. The final stroke surprised no one.

Octavius learned the truth from the servant his instructor had shouted at and certainly buggered and maybe even loved.

The frightened boy brought Octavius his master's copy of *The Republic*, inscribed to Fidus, the faithful, a dog-soldier.

It was in Greek so Octavius never read it.

The same boy told him that Pausonias had climbed into a hot bath, locked the door and cut his wrists.

Perhaps it was the death of a true Stoic.

Or, Octavius wonders now, had Pausonias been alone too long with the difficult questions?

Too much time to think. Octavius stands, stretches, pulls on the warm Bedouin cloak he prefers to any other, and takes his evening walk to the west. He leaves behind him the vast hectares of the City and trails his own shadow. It is longest at this time of day.

As he climbs the hill to Qalaat Ibn Maan, the Ottoman castle – new in Palmyrene terms – you can see him: broad-shouldered but not tall, strong, shortish neck, curling hair still thick but grizzled. Livia says he resembles Odysseus. But only in appearance. Octavius lacks cunning or guile of any sort, which means that men trust him; also that he could himself be tricked. Not too easily. Experience has made him shrewd. All the same he could never be what they call a Tivoli man, jousting for position and survival at the Villa d'Este. Politics bore him. He will never make a courtier.

The castle has been restored and made a watchtower. The sun has not yet set over the towers of the dead to the west but Otto has already lit the small fire that will be kept going all night. Electricity serves the guardhouse, as it does the principal towers in the Valley of Tombs. The fire is more cheering and warming. Otto knows the General sometimes pauses here for half an hour. He likes a chat. He must be lonely, poor sod.

'Corporal.'

'Sir.'

If the whores do come he won't be able to take advantage.

Nothing to keep the General warm but poking around for his blessed history with Lieutenant Poncy Severus. Waiting for the Savages, if only they'd show their heads. There's supposed to be an enemy, that's why we're here, but you tell me where he is. Patrol and reconnaissance reported an army once, to the south there, in the desert. But it turned out to be a sandstorm.

You could go off your head here.

'It's been a long time, hasn't it, Otto. The night before we left for Syria. You were on guard duty at the villa. We talked about action, didn't we.'

'We did, sir.'

He's not staying for a chat tonight. The General has difficulty turning his head to the right. An old wound in the neck. It bothers him more in winter.

Even when he does settle for a while by the fire and talks or listens, and sometimes you can get a laugh out of him, he'll still be looking to the west where the green runs out and the dead are. As if he can see something we can't. As if the dead could speak.

At night the sand will be cool as snow. It is pleasant already to walk though no one goes barefoot. A cobra bite is a court-martial offence, along with sunburn. Interestingly, army rules are less well-defined regarding the scorpion.

Octavius has been tempted on an evening like this when the sky hesitates between violet and indigo, day and night, to go on walking west, to put behind him all the small works of man. The desert draws him as no other place on earth. He has been to the edge and imagined the next step in the sand that would put him out of sight of Diocletian's camp, the city, Otto's comfortable fire, the sunset shouts from the watchtowers.

He contemplates this next step but hears Pausonias's dry laugh and instead turns into the tomb of the three brothers, his favourite. Octavius has his own theories about these weird sepulchres. They remind him of the Indian Towers of Silence.

He likes to think that some wanderer, far from home like him, brought the ways of the Indus to Syria and left no message.

The power flickers but Octavius can see well enough the flaking fresco of Achilles disguised as a woman: an image, so the books say, of the eternal soul robed in earthbound clothes, shed at death and set free only by death.

By the time Octavius begins his walk back to the living city it is dark. He has become a small figure in an immensity of sand. It is cold. He pulls his purple cloak around him and follows his own footprints home before they are lost in dust.

That night Severus wakes him. 'An incursion, sir. I've sent out a patrol.'

Octavius is instantly awake: a gift he has not lost through the idle years.

'Where from?'

'The south.'

'Any casualties?'

'No, sir. Just the goats.'

'Lieutenant, have you woken me to tell me that some fool has let the goats out?'

'Taken, sir. Probably the Bedouin.'

'Possibly. Report to me in the morning.'

When Severus has left, Octavius regrets his sharpness. Exile in this garrison oasis, the weary years of inaction, have made everyone jumpy. It has always been the same on frontiers but it is worse here. The enemy is there but they cannot see his face. Fantasies breed about the skill and cunning of the Savages, their barbaric ways with their victims. There are rumours of torture, cannibalism. And it is true that a few years ago a scouting expedition in a light armoured vehicle failed to return. Their transport was found but the men were not. A month later the body of one of the two was discovered by the guard patrol on the outskirts of the garrison, where the oasis gave way to sand. His tongue had been cut out, his eyes gouged and his genitals stuffed in his mouth. There had been no vehicle tracks, no print of horse or camel.

From time to time there are murmurs against the Bedouin. One conscript went mad and walked off into the desert. At night Octavius has smelled hashish from the barracks. They must get it from the Bedouin. He has done nothing about this. He is neither impotent nor condoning, merely pragmatic.

Octavius won't sleep now. No matter. He settles on a block of limestone outside his tent in the roofless Sanctuary of Bel. He will never have enough of these desert nights and feels a return of the wonder that struck him when he was fresh here.

Then, he had thought of the old Romans. Nothing in Italy, in the western empire, in the history that had been smacked into his head by tutors, had given him such a sense of that old empire, as to stand here at its eastern boundary. At Aswan, on his Egyptian posting, he had smiled at the thought of complaining Juvenal banished to that uncomfortable outpost. Here, with the desert and the Euphrates to the east, the apprehension was sharper, the connection immediate. Aurelian stood at the shoulder of Octavius.

Octavius remembers those early days. The relish, the fervour. He remembers that he felt younger than he had for years. He remembers the setting up of the garrison, the disposal of defences, the anticipation of action.

He remembers how he had paced out the ruins of this lost civilisation, read avidly, planned to restore, to dig, moleing down to the deepest history. He had kept the men busy. No hashish then.

He remembers with pleasure even that first winter when gales and rain were followed by snow from the Anti-Lebanon range and he saw golden Tadmor all frosted white, snow drifting, the worst winter for a century, the fires the men lit to keep themselves warm: the shouts, the noise, the bustle, muffled by snow. The miraculous warmth of the sulphur spring. The silence of the desert.

When the snows melted and the winter ended, the salt-flats flashed silver. The desert bloomed.

Then Octavius had the news of Paulina's birth.

He walked that spring morning down to the stream where the Bedouin women gathered. He had little Arabic, no Bedouin and he kept to the palm-grove, to his own order that the nomads should not be provoked. In particular, leave their women alone.

Octavius remembers, the women did not see him. But a small girl chasing a dog came on him in the grove. Both were startled. She appraised him with wide brown eyes. He put his finger to his lips. She grabbed the puppy and pulled it to her. Octavius thought of Paulina and wished he had something to give to this child. Then he remembered and handed over a small mark of his office, an imperial eagle brooch, tin. She snatched it and went on staring. Octavius remembered a couple of words in Arabic.

'Ish ismak?' What is your name?

'Manah,' she said, wide-eyed. Then one of the women called her name and, frightened by her own daring, she ran, the puppy yelping because she was holding it too tightly.

Octavius remembers.

3

'Facts!'

In the garden at Fiesole where his grandparents had their summer villa, Octavius's tutor, Gaius Germanicus, sighed. He had a better temper than Pausonias, later, but there were times when the boy exasperated him.

'Fidus Octavius, you are sixteen. You have every advantage in the world. So what do you find so difficult about Lucretius? The clearest of all writers. A poet for our times. What is he telling us?'

Octavius shifted on his seat. His mother's cat was sniffing the geraniums. Now it came and wound itself around his legs.

'I suppose, that religion's rubbish? That nothing exists unless we can see it?'

'Exactly! Facts! That tree is a fact. The kitten you are playing with under the table is a fact. You could say Lucretius was one of the first Existentialists. So what is your problem there?'

'I'm not sure, Gaius Germanicus. I suppose I think there must be more than that. Might be. If that's all there is to life then it seems a bit pointless.'

'Has someone been putting ideas in your head?'

'No.'

Octavius could hear his friends playing football in the old Roman theatre. The air was very clear and still. He wondered why you had to spend so much time learning things that would never be any use.

Gaius Germanicus smiled.

'Six months in the army and you'll see the pointlessness of

worrying about futility. Then you'll understand the point of Lucretius.'

The bell rang from the campanile. Not for prayer nowadays but for the hour.

How strange, Octavius has thought since that Tuscan afternoon. Pausonias would have had me a philosopher, Gaius Germanicus an Epicurean. Perhaps both were right. Certainly, it took only one campaign to teach him the exigencies of survival.

And then the joke was, re-reading Lucretius, Octavius had become convinced that the poet himself was a poor Epicurean, simply because he was a poet. His wonder at the world, his joy in marriage, the agony with which he recounted the plague that swept Athens: these were not the cold musings of tranquillity.

As he plotted his excavations in Tadmor he looked up a passage he had half in mind: 'we seem to see and hear before us men whose dead bones lie in the embrace of earth.'

'But he refutes that,' Severus had said one evening when they played chess and drank wine. 'He says such thoughts are phantasms. The sort of thing a madman would imagine.'

The General smiled.

'Then maybe I'm going mad. In any case, I take your queen.'

Facts. In the first few years there had been plenty of those. The mission was, as usual, protective and defensive. Based again on the old Roman empire, with one important difference: since the Concordia the role of the new Romans was one of peace-keeping, not conquest. The whole of the western empire looked to Tivoli to hold the southern and eastern frontiers. At the Academy the policy of Augustus and

Hadrian towards ancient Tadmor was held up as one of ideal cooperation. With the help of the Romans Tadmor was never a vassal but a free and prosperous trading state, which served at the same time as a base against Parthian threats from the East. Mark Antony's early, aggressive venture was passed over. The fall of Tadmor was attributed, fairly enough, to Zenobia.

It was an interesting speculation, though not a proven fact, that Tadmor's remarkable Queen had been taken back to Rome in golden chains and allowed to settle, with a pension, at a villa in Tivoli.

It was a fact, in those days, that Octavius had to build a living city in a dead one. The modern town of Palmyra had been sacked long ago. Octavius made use of the stones of the ancient city and wood was brought through the mountains from Lebanon, marble from Italy the following spring, and by the first full summer the barrack block was completed close to what had been the highway through the city, with access to the springs.

Octavius chose to ride a white Arab mare around the encampment, the gift of the Bedouin chief. He was a seasoned General, a figure who commanded respect. The men wiped their smiles from their faces. Many of the legion had served under him before. Fidus Octavius rarely raised his voice but he missed nothing. The rest of the officers took to horses. A stable was built up the remains of Diocletian's camp. The first year, in companies of three, the men were required to survive a week in the desert and if you hadn't listened at the briefings, you didn't come back. Someone – probably that fool Flaminius – started a joke. What has seven legs and a balls-ache? A general on a horse with a stiff prick. Whoever repeated that got the rough side of Otto's tongue and a week working the salt flats. No one laughed at the General.

No one laughed at the Bedouin either. That was orders. Octavius made a ceremony of visiting the chief, Hatim. He went on foot, unarmed, to the black tent and was received and entertained. A bargain was struck. Goats were bought and sheep promised. There would be a daily supply of unleavened bread. In season there would be dates and other fruit. After rain Hatim sent in truffles from the desert. Octavius was satisfied enough.

That was before the voices.

Before Octavius took to walking every evening in the Valley of Tombs.

Nearly dawn. Severus will be here soon. There will be the matter of the goats and the Bedouin to deal with. Octavius must be careful. He has worked hard to stay on good terms with the Bedouin. But he knows the men are looking for trouble there. Lack of action has made them restless. They need an enemy and, so far as they are concerned, an Arab is an Arab. Perhaps he has been wrong to prohibit fraternisation. Lieutenant Probus thinks so. But the Bedouin themselves are proud and touchy. And in one respect, the men could be right: there might be spies among them.

He thinks: I was too hard on Severus last night. He was right to wake me. The disappearance of the goats is not in itself sinister but there have been too many such incidents lately. The Savages may be conducting a war of nerves.

Savages? How long have I been thinking of them in such terms?

The last relief came about five years ago. Two officers left with it and in their place Severus and Probus arrived.

Octavius enjoys the company of his two young lieutenants. Severus is tall, thin, well-educated, with a sensitivity to the occasions upon which rank must be respected or may be put aside.

When he first arrived he was a little shy of the General. Probably scared, fresh from the Academy, unlike Probus who had come up from the ranks and seen action.

Chess helped to cure that, and wine. And the baths they shared in the sulphur spring. Gradually, Severus put aside deference and began to talk freely. He had an easy blush and features that might be called delicate. Before Probus joined them in the baths, Octavius guessed that there would be gossip about his relationship with the young lieutenant. He was not concerned. The idea amused him faintly. He had never loved a man but was there not a woman in every man, a man in every woman? He knew what went on in the barracks and doubted if there was much love there, though perhaps there was. There had been homosexuality at the Academy, of course, even though such habits had been outlawed by the great new Roman empire. The Greek way was the derogatory euphemism for such relationships, punishable by dishonourable discharge. On the frontiers it was a matter left to the discretion of the commanding officer.

Whenever anyone referred to the Greek way, Octavius thought of Pausonias and the tears in the eyes of the boy who brought him the Macedonian's posthumous present. He was too young then to have thought of it but he hoped someone looked after the boy, once Pausonias had given his last shrug and left.

Octavius did not know if Severus was homosexual. He did not care.

Severus had read as much as Livia, a lot more than Octavius. And with Octavius he shared a passion for the buried life of the strange place to which they were condemned.

Octavius blinked and towelled his eyes. The sulphur was malodorous. It made him weep. And yet it was the source of life.

At first, he saw this as wonderful: a blessed oasis in an implacable desert. No wonder the Bedouin hated the sun and loved water.

Later, by the time he has taken to his walks among the towers, Octavius is possessed by other intimations; if you are looking for a picture of human life, here is this small patch of green. You take a drink, rest in the shade, and then it is time to go. In such a mood he begins to see the gesture of Pausonias as gallant.

But then, before the mysterious silence from Tivoli, when the years had not yet piled up, Severus admitted that he had found shortcomings in the Academy's system of instruction.

'I mean, it's all right if you don't ask questions. The whole thing is organised to discourage you from thinking for yourself. That turns out good soldiers. It suits most people.'

Octavius nodded. He reached for the jug of cold water, poured half over himself and passed the jug to Severus.

'But you?'

'Well, take Tadmor. The Augustinian pax. Hadrian. All fair enough. They protected the city. But then they destroyed it. No one ever talks about that.'

'What else could Aurelian have done? The Palmyrenes slaughtered his garrison.'

Severus shrugged.

'The way they teach you at the Academy – it's so black and white. No room for greys. All the empires after Rome were evil. Upright Rome. Rome the just and even-handed, brought down by barbarians.'

Severus suddenly realised to whom he was speaking. He blushed.

'I'm sorry, sir.'

Octavius smiled.

'What for? We're both naked, Severus. No rank in here. You'd look a damnfool saluting me.' When Octavius studied Severus his thoughts turned to Rufus, the same age, not unlike him in build. 'But you did well at the Academy.'

'In the end. It would have been stupid not to. But I nearly got chucked out in my second year.'

'I didn't know that. What for?'

'Reading Catullus. Translating a bit. You know, the Greek influence, anti-Caesar, generally subversive.'

'Didn't he live at Tivoli?'

'Yes, among other places.'

'Funny. Tivoli keeps coming up. I've never read Catullus.'

'I could lend you my copy. There's one I looked up when we came here. I can't remember the exact words but it's about going to Asia Minor, leaving home. How you want to go but you're nervous too. He's saying goodbye to his friends.'

'Poets and soldiers. Both must leave home, I suppose. Tell me, Severus, why did you come here? Your father's in the Military Command, I know him. You could have picked your posting.'

'I applied, sir. I was interested in Tadmor of course.' Severus spoke hesitantly. 'And then there was the frontier – the idea of the frontier. I wanted to go the edge. I suppose that sounds foolish.'

'Not to me.' Octavian thought. 'Well, we'd better get back. Lieutenant, I'm thinking of looking into the history here, maybe a bit of digging, though I'm no archaeologist. Even some restoration, if we're here long enough. Would you like to help?'

'Yes, sir. Very much.'

Severus stood and pulled a towel around his waist. He stood so easily, no stiff bones there, the young man's body was still his friend. Nowadays Octavius had that feeling of fluid movement – almost of release from gravid flesh – only when he rode his white mare, Dido, the great present from Chief Hatim.

'You remind me of someone, Severus.'

'Sir?'

Rufus, why did you turn away?

My son, my blame.

The stink of sulphur had got into his throat. The sweat streamed from his forehead. Octavius mopped his eyes.

That was years ago. Octavius calls for water to shave and then sees, it is already at his elbow. In summer, when he sleeps in a tent in the Sanctuary of Bel, he hangs a small mirror from the tent-frame.

Livia used to say that I was a centaur. In part, because of my passion for horses. Not that I was ever one of the Villa d'Este crowd who chattered and gambled every Sunday at the curriculum equorum. I didn't judge them. It was all part of the political game and the absence of the Commander of the Praetorian Guard was certainly noticed and noted. But even if I had wished to take part, this was a game I would have played badly. I don't have what they call charm or social ease so I let them laugh at me as a plain soldier. By then, in any case, I reckoned that I was at the end of my career.

I did not relish watching horses race, sometimes break their hearts, literally, for a bet, obeying a jockey who, in turn, has his own master. I liked to see horses run free. And I liked to ride them. If I had stayed in Tivoli I had plans for stables.

And then Livia said I was a centaur because when I was mounted I looked not like a horseman but a horse-man. I am even built a little like a horse, she says. If that is so, then I'm no Arab, like Dido, but a sturdy work-horse, made not for grace but stamina. Rufus must get his slimness, his ease with his body, from Livia. My legs and torso are strong but Rufus will be taller than me by now. A Roman head, says Livia, whatever that is. What I see in the mirror is a heavy skull, a wide face and mouth, a nose that fits the face.

Livia insisted that I submit to a sculptor. That was some years ago in Alexandria. I finally bargained that in return, she would sit for her portrait.

In the bronze head I do not recognise myself but I daresay that is always the case with portraiture. So, once over my embarrassment, I looked at the features of a vaguely familiar stranger. Who is he? He has an air of a practical soldier. But also, in the eyes, of almost foolish openness: hardly innocence, surely? But the expression of someone who is gazing at something a great distance away. A great illumination or a great horror. Whatever it is about this stranger, he accepts.

But I treasure the miniature of Livia the artist took for me from the larger portrait. He caught her exactly. Not prettiness but the beauty of intelligence and courage in her high forehead, straight nose, wide-set eyes, lips full but not smiling. She looks as she does when she does not know she is observed. It is the fashion of the day, to present the subject as a figure from antiquity; so Livia's is a face from the Villa of Mysteries at Pompeii. At first, I thought nothing of this. Later, now, I take out the miniature and see a woman who died a long time ago, petrified in an instant of ordinary life. There have been worse deaths than that catastrophe in the aeons of history since; and yet I cannot bear the thought of this one woman.

And then there is another picture I saw somewhere, of a brown-eyed young man, a boy, sensuous nostrils and mouth, wearing the laurel, looking out straight at the painter from a smile (an invitation?). The portrait came from Egypt but it could be any boy. He might be looking at his reflection in a mirror. A little of Rufus, a little of Severus, and something of both.

I scrape at my stubble in the cracked piece of mirror-glass. I prefer sunset to sunrise. The bristle on my chin is whiter than on my head and grows with amazing vigour. The camp creaks awake. A cockerel calls. A donkey answers: ha brou ha. A few men are trudging back from their nightwatch in the Valley of Tombs. There are a few vague smells: cooking, animals, the acrid air men make together when they live without women.

It was a few months before Probus joined Octavius and Severus in the sulphur bath.

He did not come often and when he did was never truly at ease. Unlike Severus he had risen from the ranks, commissioned in the field on the Egyptian border with Libya. He was short and wiry, his face weathered, his body hard. Octavian saw Probus as an outstandingly loyal and capable officer but a somewhat lonely figure banished from the company of men like Otto yet never quite at home in the officers' mess.

So far as Probus was concerned, a naked General was a General still. When he joined Octavius and Severus in the sulphur baths he never initiated conversation. He never took off his towel. Octavius began to wonder if he had been clumsy ever to invite Probus.

And then, interestingly, when Severus did not turn up one evening, Probus relaxed a little.

Octavius asked him about his campaigns and Probus answered.

'And do you have family, Lieutenant?'

'Wife and two children, sir. In Rome.'

'You miss them? They must miss you?'

'We're all used to it, sir.'

'And what do you make of this posting?'

There was a connection between the two of them. An understanding? Something not possible when Severus was present.

'I've known many worse, sir.'

'But?'

Probus wiped his brow with his forearm. He sweated more than Severus.

'Well, sir, I'd always go for a strike before frontier defence but nowadays there's not much choice. I manage, it's my job. But if there isn't a relief soon we might have trouble with the men.'

'We keep them busy. You mean they want action? That's what Otto says.'

'Not so much that. It's this queer place. The desert. If they could even see the face of the enemy. Some of them think there's no one there, not even Savages.'

'That's what they call them?'

'Yes, sir.'

'Any suggestions, Probus?'

'I'd let them mix more with the Bedouin. Up to a point. Defuse suspicion. Lower the temperature.'

'Until a Bedouin girl gets pregnant. I'll think about it, Probus. You like them, don't you?'

'The Bedouin? Yes, sir.'

Octavian sensed that was enough of questions. Thus far and no further, Probus seemed to say. You are there and I am here and that is the order of things.

That night Octavius wrote in the personal journal he kept locked up with his official log.

I love this place. The golden pillars. The palms. In the Sanctuary of Bel where I have my summer quarters, there is an astrological ceiling in the north adyton. The god himself, Bel or Jupiter, is a repeated figure in the cupola. From here he seems to control the twelve signs of the Zodiac and outside that an eagle among stars. Until she was obliged to turn her head to the West it appears that Tadmor looked to the East. So this faith in a divinely controlled destiny through which the heavenly will works by means of the stars, may well have crossed the Euphrates from Mesopotamia, from the Garden of Eden itself.

And then I walk out at night, just far enough to leave behind me the fires and lights of the encampment, and I look up and see as the ancients did, this multitude of stars. We know that they are not fixed in the heavens, that many are dead, we are admiring dead light; but for that time I have no difficulty in understanding what they knew. That there is an order to everything.

In Africa I have seen the Southern Cross.

I am neither an astrologer nor an astronomer. I don't even know the names of these stars beyond the obvious ones, the Plough and the Milky Way and Orion's Belt. Severus does. I must ask him.

I cannot say how I will feel if we are here too long. If Tivoli forgets us, if I am away from Livia for ever, no doubt my feelings about this place will change.

Yet it will be something that there were a few summer nights when I stood in simple wonder at those cold white fires in the sky, some shading to blue, some gold, and was lifted out of my reason by this sight.

There is consolation as well as rebuke in the immensity of those desert skies. We are nothing but because we can peel back our eyes like this, we may see eternity.

I'm writing this for you, Livia. I can talk to you more comfortably here than I can in letters. You are close to me at all times but most of all in the writing of this journal. As if we were sitting either side of an olive-wood fire, simply talking. And I can see the tilt of your head, the way your eyes widen, sometimes in irony. I can almost hear your voice.

I wish you were with me. Perhaps this will be possible soon. I have written again to the Master of Soldiers. Even after five years I am still amazed at this place. Did I tell you, I am very pleased with my new lieutenants. I'm turning into an amateur archaeologist. Severus is digging at the site of the old museum and today he found something. I think I said in my last letter, if you got it, to tell Gaius Germanicus that I have started on Lucretius again.

In my letters I tell you not to worry about Rufus. But of course you do, and so do I. Here, I'll confess that I blame myself.

How I long to see Paulina. It's hard to believe she is five. The day I had the news of Paulina's baptism (now that is something I could not put in a letter!) I first saw the Bedouin child, Manah. I came across her again today, with the women at the stream. She must be about twelve now. It's sad, in a way, when they lose their guilelessness, but entertaining, too. She was wearing a red skirt that looked new and instead of running to me as she used to, she snatched a veil over the lower part of her face, though watching me still with those big brown eyes. She was flirting, although I don't think she knew what she was doing.

I have discovered her name, Manah, means destiny.

In the years since, Octavius has kept up his journal, although it is less for Livia now, more for himself.

There is the matter of the missing goats to be dealt with.

Octavius scrapes at the last of his stubble and wonders, if he grew a beard, would it be white? The risen sun flashes in the mirror, dazzling him. He blinks.

Otto again.

I reckon the Bedouin took the goats. I mean, the Savages couldn't have got past the guard. No one would think much of a Bedouin even though they're not supposed to come into the encampment, they do. We use them as herdsmen and to look after the beasts. And we never count them. If a few of them had taken off into the desert or the mountains, we wouldn't know. They're supposed to be nomads anyhow. They only stay around Tadmor because they do well out of us. It's like fleas on a dog.

Mind you, things have got a bit slack. Twice I've caught one of the guards asleep on duty lately. They got what was coming to them but that doesn't solve the problem. It comes from the top if you ask me. First, you've got a lot of men too long without women or action. Then there's the General. He's got respect, he'd never lose that, but he's in a queer state of mind. The early years, there was no stopping him. He was everywhere, checking on defences, the building, sending out patrols and reconnaissance sorties, digging after his history. He looked younger than the time he first spoke to me when I was doing guard duty at the Tivoli villa.

I saw him a few times just standing in the desert, grinning up at the stars.

Now it's as if he isn't here, not with us, in an ordinary everyday way. Something funny about his eyes as though he was looking at something we couldn't see. Or at nothing.

And he doesn't know the half of what goes on in the barracks. I'm not going to be the one to tell him that Flaminius will serve anyone any way they like, provided it's in the arse. Quite a fancy whore he looks when he's done himself up in skirts and face stuff. Not for me but I've got to admit in a bad light you wouldn't know the difference. If the whores come yesterday it won't be too soon. And the Bedouin sell them hashish and when they've smoked enough Flaminius looks like the most beautiful virgin girl on earth.

But Flaminius is sick. He's got some poxy scabs. Without Flaminius and without their smokes I wouldn't be responsible for anything they did. Seeing that Tivoli's written us off.

I'm a regular. I take it as it comes.

I know the men have made up their minds, they didn't have to think. I do think. But they want to believe the Bedouin stole the goats. Because otherwise it has to be the Savages.

Octavius decides to go on foot to see old Hatim, just as he did the first time they met.

'What do you think, Probus?'

'I'd say he might be offended, sir. He gave you four legs. He'd be insulted if you arrived on two.'

'Yes, you're right. Get someone to saddle Dido. How is the old man?'

'Not too good but he won't admit it. I think it's his stomach. I offered to send our surgeon but he won't have it. Perhaps you can persuade him, sir?'

'I doubt that.'

A certain ceremony was always involved in meetings with the Bedouin chief. In the early years Octavius enjoyed visiting Hatim, sitting by the fire. Even without a common language there had been respect between the two men.

Then Probus had arrived. He spoke some Arabic and soon learned to understand the Bedouin dialect. At the same time

Octavius realised that for Hatim this was a meeting between chiefs, involving a banquet the Bedouin could not afford. At the least, a sheep slaughtered.

Today there is no question of banquets.

Hatim knows why they have come. He is standing outside his tent, a thin figure. Octavius, Probus and Severus dismount. The women watch from a short distance away. They are frankly curious, brightly dressed, unveiled. One of them laughs. Octavius glimpses a red skirt. The camels are not hobbled. They will not stray.

Courtesies are exchanged but are not drawn out.

Hatim's thinness is no longer that of strength and hard life but frailty.

It is still early but the pinky-blue of dawn has been sucked into the white heat of the sky. Even figures as close as the women shake in the light. One detaches herself from the others. They could be smoke. Octavius used to love this desert. He is still drawn to it but increasingly sees these sands as regions of mirage and phantasm. He could be struck dumb here, the sun could burn out his eyes.

Probus is talking.

Hatim says he has heard of the loss of the goats.

The women are moving back towards Hatim's tent, impelled by curiosity. One is the most daring. She is taking form out of smoke.

The chief offers his goats to the General.

Tell him, of course not. We thank him.

The three soldiers look heavy, cumbered in this heat. They sweat. Hatim is dry, armoured as a locust, friable. He could return to powder, sand, smoke.

'If my people have taken your goats, may Allah strike my sons.'

'Tell him, we ask only if he has seen a thief.'

'Count my goats. We have the numbers. The General knows the numbers. We are blind in our sleep to thieves. The General was my brother.'

Octavius sees glaucoma in Hatim's milky eyes.

'Tell him, I am always his brother.'

'Then why does the General come with these words? They are stones in my ears. I shall call my daughter who has charge of the goats. The General may count them.'

Severus murmurs: 'I don't think we're getting anywhere.'

'What is he saying?'

'He's calling his daughter to bring the goats.'

'He says there are jinn. They are demons who live in the regions we do not know. They go to live in men's heads to send them mad. They become wild animals who will eat a whole herd.'

Hatim is still talking, wildly it appears, raising his narrow hands in imprecation, a plaiting gesture. He might be praying or cursing.

'I think he is saying the Savages are jinn.'

The General sighs. Hatim is wailing on. Now he points. The sky has turned from dirty white to pewter. A sudden wind (has he called it up?) rattles anything standing in the camp, snatches at the black tents. At Hatim's dusty robe. Long ago the General gave permission for the wearing of Arab headdress, the kiffayah. Although he pulls it across his mouth he can already taste sand. It is a hot wind, from the desert, from the east.

Dido gives a whinny of complaint, dances where she stands.

But this is only a warning. The wind drops, leaving the air yellowish, opaque. The General blinks. There is a smell of dung and hashish about the camp. Motes of sand in the air take the shape of a girl driving black goats before her.

Probus says: 'Hatim asks you to count them.'

The three soldiers back away from the bleating goats. They are in danger of being surrounded.

The girl who drives them wears a red skirt. Gold coins jangle at her neck. Her head is uncovered, her hair long, black and tangled, shiny with something. She was seven or so, down by the stream, the day Octavius heard that Paulina had been christened. Octavius gave her a tin brooch, the eagle. She was seven or so, putting on the airs of a woman. She is grown now, still very young, but a girl, not a child.

This is Manah, the daughter of Hatim.

The General smiles.

'I give in. Tell him to call off the goats. I am his brother. I trust my brother with my life.'

Probus frowns.

'Hatim says you have a son and a daughter. Would you trust him to be their father?'

'I would.'

'Then you are as a father to his sons and his daughter. So his goats are your goats.'

Laughter from a sand-dry throat is painful. It could also give offence.

'Tell him, peace be with him.'

'And he wishes you peace. And sons to stand at your shoulder. And daughters to bless your house.'

The General steps forward. The old chief embraces him. Octavius feels twice the brush of a papery cheek on his face.

The Bedouin's breath is thin against Octavius's face. It is drawn with some effort from an exhausted frame. The General would like to be free to mourn Hatim.

Dido is fussing at the bit. She smells the wind coming back.

The three soldiers ride away.

Octavius looks back once, reining in Dido. He sees Hatim still standing there: a scribbled figure, a wand.

At midday the promised sandstorm sweeps in from the east. Before the wind rises there is a thickening of the air. Breathing is difficult.

The mountains disappear and then the Towers of the Dead. The animals cry out, horses are restless in their stalls.

Quieting Dido, Octavius feels under his hand the long rippling shiver peculiar to horses. And the smell of her, he knows that, it is one of his consolations: when she is afraid the smell is different. She snatches her head away as though pulling at an invisible martingale and dances and dances, and calls to and answers the other horses. They kick at their stalls, iron on wood.

Normally in such weather Octavius would abandon his summer tent and join the other officers at Diocletian's Camp in a low stone building on the site of the old Castra Romana. When he first built there the General had had the idea of restoring the magnificent tetrapylon. He had had so many ideas then. In those days he saw archaeology and restoration as works of continuity: affirmations of the common humanity that runs through the muddle of history. He had not expected to be long at Tadmor. He was in a hurry.

Today Octavius makes an eccentric decision to sit out this weather. He wants to see if he can survive it. He sees himself, like stone, as eroded and weathered, both.

Besides, only in such weather can he be alone with his ruined city. There will be guards but he cannot see them.

Soon, he can see no further than arm's length. Then, as the wind comes up, he is blind. The tent has been folded before the wind can take it. Octavius makes a tent of his cloak, pulls the scarf around his face and closes his eyes against the sand. By touch he finds his way to a corner of the Temple of Bel and huddles there.

But there is no illumination. Nothing beyond the enduring. His teeth are gritty, they will be stripped white by the flying sand.

There is no one there. Nothing but the punishing wind-sand. No Savages. No Livia. No past, no present, no history. But the skull not quite scoured clean. I can hear the thin voice of Hatim's dying. In this storm the boundary between city and desert is lost. It was fragile at the best of times, like the line between life and death. Hatim will cross it easily, perhaps in this world of sand the last exhalation will be no more than a puff that lets the spirit free from its cage of bone. So brave and hungry and angry and loving, that vivid flesh. And then dust. Gaius Germanicus, a true new Roman, smiled fatly in the Tuscan afternoon and said: 'this is all there is but is it not enough?' Lucretius says the same but he puts it better. I cannot remember. I have come late to words.

And Pausonias. Are you there? I can hear your mocking voice, I hear it often nowadays. It was one of the first voices. Now you are so long gone we have a dialogue at last. You say, why am I hiding like this? There is nothing to be afraid of but fear. You made that crossing from city to desert voluntarily, casually. Gallantly.

Octavius struggles to his feet. Pausonias is right. What is the point of staying out in the storm if you hide?

So he walks, stumbles, his arm with the cloak held up before him to break the force of the wind. With the other arm he flails for balance and touch.

I understand now about jinns. The sandstorm is not like a curtain but something living, changing. The motes rush together to form phantoms. The wind spirals and there is a girl. She wears a dusty red skirt and coins at her throat and her forehead. I stagger a few steps and reach out for her. I call her name: Manah. But there is no one there. Or there was a demon.

These storms usually blow for three days. If I had the courage to follow Pausonias and to make that crossing, by the time they found me I would be free.

Walking around in a sandstorm: Commander of the Garrison, General of the Legion, have you gone mad?

Octavius laughs, grazes his hand.

How long have I been here? Is it night? In the end, Pausonias, can laughter save you?

'General?'

I am falling.

'Severus? Is that you?'

'Otto, sir. Give me your arm. Easy does it.'

I told you, didn't I? He's had this queer look lately. Lieutenant Probus was worried so we both set out to look for him. And there he was staggering around, blind with sweat and sand. Laughing. Couldn't see the joke myself.

I didn't need to be told to keep this to myself. The men still think a lot of him. So do I. I'd follow him anywhere. Whatever had got into his head, he's all right now. Cut his hand, that's all. And the skin of his face broken by the flying grit. Could have lost an eye.

Of course, you have to understand, we've got grievances, he's got worries – that's the difference.

Savages apart, there's the worry of how to get by since supplies stopped. Most of us try not to think about what's going on at home. We don't always manage it. There was the man who just walked off into the desert. He was mad. But then two of them tried to leg it through the mountains. They never came back. No idea if they made it.

Then they say Hatim's on the way out. They were close in the old days. The General would walk to the camp in the evenings or ride out on Dido and sit with the chief for hours. Don't ask me what language they talked but they got on. He'll miss the smelly old bugger. That could be preying on his mind. He's only human.

I am sitting out the night. It is strange to be in my winter quarters in summer. We use the generator only sparingly nowadays so I asked for an oil lamp and I find it gives a kind light. I washed as well as I could but it will take a sulphur bath to get rid of the sand. I am a sand-man.

It was absurd and irresponsible, that testing I gave myself. If the Savages do strike, this is exactly the weather they would choose. They could cross the line from the desert into the oasis invisibly. They could be taken for creatures of hallucination, sand-devils.

It is important that we do not give them the stature of monsters but over the years that is what they have become, because we have never seen them.

Probus had already doubled the guard, exactly what I would have done myself. I can trust him. I trust Severus too, but Probus is the practical one. He takes the facts and acts on them. In that he resembles the soldierly part of me.

I am out of my madness now, if that is what it was. They will wake me if they need me but I have already decided not to sleep.

Perhaps this is an indulgence but not a serious one. I have made up my mind to sit out a nightwatch for Hatim. It is hard to breathe. This storm will surely take him.

When I first came and met Hatim I made a few notes about the Bedouin. I wrote to Livia that their women are more like gypsies in appearance. I am not good with words but I told her that in my longing to see Paulina I had noticed the girl, Manah and watched her through the years.

I said, I think I frightened the child. To these people we must look so white and heavy, so old. They are sharp and quick, thin, all nerves and sinew. They eat dates and a mixture of flour, or roasted corn, with water or milk. They have a law of hospitality, which meant that I had to visit Hatim less often. Each time a feast would be made for me. They play an instrument like a flute, made of wood.

It is interesting that some have gone back to the old gods of the desert. Not that they ever paid total service to Islam. And if any faith makes sense here, it is surely animism: the moon, the sun, the rain for their palm-groves and modest crops; but most of all the King of gods Bal or Bel who is the chief spirit of this miraculous spring of Tadmor, without whom there would be no oasis, no life, no history?

One of my greatest fears is that the men will confuse the

Bedouin with the Savages. For that reason I followed Probus's advice and for a time allowed a degree of fraternisation with the Bedouin. That came to an end when one of the men took to meeting a Bedouin girl in an abandoned funerary tower. They are not Savages. Unusually, Hatim came to me, with ceremony and his sons at his side. I could tell the men saw them as barbarians in rags as they made their way through the garrison mounted on camels, but Otto made sure that no one laughed.

So Hatim asked me to punish him the man. I did so, in a way the Bedouin could understand, with twenty lashes. Afterwards, Hatim sent me a tribute.

Livia, my darling, I can only pretend to talk to you. The mail has stopped and we can get no answer from Tivoli. The lines might well be down but even on the radio telephone there is no reply. It is a mysterious and disturbing silence, all the more since we are running low on fuel. I am afraid for you. Were we indiscreet in our letters? Rumours reached us of plots at Tivoli. Have they made you pay for the baptism of Paulina, your contempt for the Villa d'Este? Don't trust Gaius Germanicus too much. How I wish Rufus were with you. Do you remember the ponds by the ruined temple when I was at the Academy? That was the day Pausonias said I'd never learn Greek. You are so clever, so quick. I am pewter to your gold.

I'm sure of one thing: you are alive. If you were not, I would know. In this stone room by the soft lamp I smell your skin, I talk to you because I must stay awake.

After all, I slept. It is dawn. The silence woke me. The storm has blown itself out. In the night the goats were mysteriously returned. I fell asleep with my head on the table, a glass of wine spilled. My neck aches from the wound in Africa, my eyes are gummy with sand.

Hatim went in the night. Easily, they tell me. I can see

those narrow yellow hands in that strange plaiting gesture as if he were drawing down a golden cord from heaven. It is a perfect morning. I can hear the Bedouin women wailing and the black goats crying out.

4

Hello. Otto.

Quite a time we're having. It's a week since the sandstorm and the business of the goats. I was telling the General, the men still say it was the Bedouin that took them. I reckoned things were getting very tricky, what with the heat and the boredom.

Then they tell us: the whores are really coming. Lieutenant Probus fixed it. Don't ask me how. But he could see how things were. He was one of us once, wasn't he. That'll put Flaminius's nose out of joint and not just his nose.

For myself I'm not sure. They may be clean or not. My trouble is I can't get that Bedouin girl out of my head, the one in the red skirt.

And then there is the new arrival. He staggered into the Bedouin camp half-dead and they brought him to us. His face was burned black and we thought at first he was blind. They've put him in the winter quarters, under guard, but I'd say he's one of us. Lieutenant Severus has been trying to get him to talk. Maybe he will if he lives, poor sod.

I usually look on the bright side but I've got to say, even if the whores come that's not the answer. I thought of talking to the General but in the end I told Probus, ever since the goats were stolen and returned, it's got worse. The men blame the Bedouin because the whole thing has given them the creeps. There's talk that the Savages are moving in on us, quite close. They're watching. It's as if they could make themselves invisible.

I said to Lieutenant Probus, whatever the risk, we've got to go out and find them or it'll be mutiny or wholesale desertion into the mountains.

I don't credit half the stories about the Savage. That he eats human flesh, that he screws anything on two or four legs, that he drinks the menstrual blood of his women, that he can see on the darkest night, that he's got a tail and two heads and can ride for a week without sleep.

All I say is, if we could catch one and slit his throat and bring his body back, we'd have a legion again instead of a bunch of half-crazed wankers.

That's all we need, I said to Lieutenant Probus. To see his face.

This is a voice you haven't heard before. I have to think what to say.

I'm sorry. The circumstances are difficult, as I'm sure you will understand.

I shall tell you what happened so far as I can, but first I have to order my thoughts.

The people we are with are kind. They have put themselves into danger for us. I try to hide my fears and the blame I put on myself and my loss. Not to dream of Fidus Octavius and so wake expecting to find the imprint of his head on the pillow beside me, for then I cannot always check the tears and my daughter cries too, without quite knowing why.

Let me give you the simple picture. It is midsummer, hot, very beautiful at dawn and at dusk in these hills. In the evenings I walk through the olive grove. The day, except for the siesta, is mercifully filled with small tasks. We milk the goats. We make white cheese, straining it through muslin bags. We dare not put out our laundry to dry on the bushes so instead we hang it indoors and the clean blue smell is not unpleasant.

I have a few books with me but the day is too occupied for reading and at night by candlelight the print blurs, the book falls to the floor.

By day my daughter seems happy enough. Our friends spoil

her. She likes the chickens and the puppy. She lives regardless in that world of story all children inhabit, making up her own intricate universe. And yet she has nightmares. Terrible dreams. Inconsolable, she is then, as if she knew everything.

By day she brings me a brown egg found in the brambles, stones, flowers, treasures, gifts. As though she were the one responsible for my peace. She is childish for her years but also too old.

I should have known better than to trust anyone in Tivoli.

The friend who brought us here told me that the new regime at the Villa d'Este has cut off all communication with the Syrian outpost. I can only think they mean to isolate them and let them perish, for reasons of their own.

I have got brown, tanned. My hands are rough. I welcome the hard work, the blisters, the way the softness has fallen from my body, so I am strong.

Perhaps I should tell you my name. It is Livia.

Strangely, as Tivoli recedes and darkness and silence close around it, for Octavius his life there grows increasingly vivid, takes on fresh colour, sound and scent. As if he were an old man, dozing out the end of his years.

So there is the boy, swimming in the same pool from which later he was to see Livia. The leaves of the ilex grove, which marked the boundary between the girls' pool and the boys', are olive-coloured, silvery underneath, the bark like an elephant's hide.

In the sulphur baths young Severus wants to talk about the new Roman ethic, the sickness of the western empire.

'It was the same with the ancients. The disease from within left the empire weak. Civil war. Usurpers. Rebellious garrisons on frontiers like this.'

Fidus Octavius nods but his gaze is turned elsewhere. He looks inward and sees himself, yawning with friends through the tutorials of Gaius Germanicus. There is the waxy smell of the desks. On the board Gaius Germanicus has written: Strength without Force. Power without Greed. Justice. Peace.

Outside the school-room there is a courtyard, an atrium. In the centre an orange tree. The boys steal the fruit but they are bitter. They steal them all the same.

On the wall there are two maps. On one, deserts are coloured a cheerful yellow. Most of the African continent is yellow. Last week they had to write an essay about the migration north of the dying peoples of Africa. For all but defence the sunset sands of the Mahgreb are lost to man. Then there is Arabia Perdita.

There are in the African territories just a few spots marked green, where the rain falls enough to be noted and as a man, Octavius will one day receive a harsh but not fatal wound in the neck.

The second, political, map of the new Roman empire colours the world pink from the frozen ice floes of the north to the western Atlantic seaboard, south to the Indian Ocean and east to the Euphrates: a boundary that has, since Octavius's youth, retreated to Tadmor.

Octavius quite likes colouring in the maps. Today however, is one of the three classes a week of Old Roman Studies, compulsory throughout the empire, vital for entrance to the Academy.

Octavius yawns. He can hear a woman singing. A dog barks.

Meanwhile Gaius Germanicus has eyes in the back of his head and a ruler in his hand. He is talking about some old poet. Octavius is dreaming of the deep green pond, the silky chill of the first dive on a hot afternoon, the mystery of the ancient spring that gives the pool life.

It is supposed to be bottomless. The boys make it a dare to swim as deep as they can hold their breath. Deeper. Today they are diving to settle the Victor, who will be crowned with a laurel wreath and keep his title for a year. Of course, it would be easy to cheat. Just to stay underwater long enough. It is a matter of honour not to cheat. *Honestas*. That's another of the words

Gaius Germanicus and the other Latin tutor, Diodorus, are so keen on. Not to be confused with *honos*, which is an official distinction, earned and bestowed. *Honestas* is a moral virtue.

Octavius remembers himself as, characteristically, neither the cleverest boy nor the most stupid.

His mind can wander but that is normal. He is unlikely to get academic *honos* but he understands about moral virtue: what they call the Roman way. At this age his mind is more receptive to facts than to ideas. He is good at dates. He finds Caesar's Gallic Wars boring but he plods through. As a very young child he used to enjoy the book of stories for children his mother read to him. Especially, he used to ask for the Adventures of Aeneas. Not all that stuff about Dido or the gods but the battles; and how Aeneas left burning Ilium with his father on his shoulders.

Now Octavius is having to transcribe Virgil he sees that the infants' story-book started with the same line: *I sing of warfare and a man at war*.

He never saw his father. He died at the hands of the Savages in one of the last Arabian wars.

Octavius knew from an early age that he would be a soldier. That was not an idea but a fact.

Gaius Germanicus's rule cracks down on Octavius's knuckles.

'Fidus Octavius! Are you listening?'

'Sir? Yes, sir.'

'Then you can tell us: for whom was Horace writing?'

'Augustus, sir. The Emperor.'

'And what was the name of Augustus before he was Emperor?'

Octavius wonders why you can't just be a soldier. What does poetry have to do with anything? Time goes very slowly after the tutor's question. An orange falls from the tree. My mother cries sometimes but only when she thinks I can't hear. My knuckles hurt but pain is not supposed to matter.

'I don't know, sir.'

'You don't know your own name? Before he was Emperor the name of Augustus was Octavian. You bear an honourable name. And can you give us a single title, I wonder, from Horace's Epodes?'

Another dreadful pause.

'*Horrida tempestas*?'

'And what does that mean?'

'A horrible tempest?'

Gaius Germanicus had half-hoped to catch him out. There are times when he is irritated by Fidus Octavius: that clear-eyed look. With schoolboys he is used to guile and tricks. Is Fidus laughing at him behind that open gaze? Or could the boy be exactly what he appears, no more, no less?

Two years from now, in the Fiesole garden, working with Fidus Octavius to cram him for the Academy entrance, Gaius Germanicus will glimpse not a cleverer but a more reflective aspect to his pupil's mind. Not many sixteen-year-olds argue about Lucretius.

For the moment Gaius Germanicus has enough to do. To get a class of pubescent boys through the raunchy Epodes and on to the safer Odes.

'Very well. Now let us continue, with the permission of Fidus Octavius. *At, o deorum*. Who can tell me the meaning of *at* in this context?'

The younger boys are out. They are using the fallen orange as a ball. Finally, Gaius Germanicus dismisses his class. There is the clatter of desk-lids, the rush to be gone. Gaius Germanicus wipes the board, sighs and eases the weight of the spectacles on the bridge of his nose. The tutor does not question his occupation. He is serving the new Roman empire in the way for which he is best equipped, he knows that. The empire requires a certain kind of citizen, especially among the élite of Tivoli, most of whom will go on to the Academy and the army or to the Civil Service. So far as he can, Gaius Germanicus steers young minds in the right direction. He also performs from time to time small services for the Villa d'Este which he hopes will not go unnoticed when the matter of his pension is settled.

In the atrium the older boys have joined the children and one has seized the orange. There is a yell. The orange has burst, spilling its red blood on the marble.

Gaius sighs and turns.

'Fidus? I thought you had all gone. Is there something you don't understand?'

'That poem, sir. Why did they believe in gods?'

'Because they were afraid.'

In the sulphur bath the General feels the heaviness of his head. That foolishness in the sandstorm has left him weary. He puts his hand to knead and ease the familiar pain from the old wound in his neck. It is an unconscious gesture but Severus has noticed. Through all the years the lieutenant has become in part the son Rufus might have been, then in the femininity of his perceptions in part a wife. Not of the flesh, of course. Never of the flesh. But here we have neither sons nor daughters nor wives and there are those who make accommodations. Severus is beautiful, I can see that; and he is careless of his beauty, he would be generous but he does not knowingly seduce. Slim, eyes the dark slanting olives of Rufus; narrow hips, golden fur, the resting sex he does not bother to cover with a towel. He has got me oils for my neck from the Bedouin. He has thin, clever hands. I thank him. My servant rubs in the oil but his touch is rough. The love between men is a chamber I have never entered, it is not my way. Nor Probus's whores, I fear, if they ever arrive. I like to think of Severus as he was when he first helped me with the excavations. That was good, those were rich, cheerful times. Getting our hands dirty, digging up history.

Since the voices, since Tivoli forgot us, since Hatim's death, I am not sure that there is any place of comfort of which a man can say with certainty: I shall never go there.

'Are the whores coming?'

Octavius has interrupted Severus in his discourse on the fall of the old Romans. The empire.

'If anyone can fix it Probus can.'

The General nods.

'When I was a boy I had a tutor called Gaius Germanicus. I think I tormented him, in a way. Did you swim in the ponds by the temple? The ilex grove?'

Severus says: 'By my time they were forbidden. A boy drowned there. Or nearly drowned. Something like that. A few still did, all the same.'

'Yes.'

Fidus Octavius stands in line to dive for the Victor's crown. Some of the others are playing around but not as much as usual. In their way they take this competition seriously. It is theirs. No adult told them to do it.

You can smell the cold of the pool even before you see it. The sun has passed its zenith but it is still hot. The ilex grove is thick. You can hear the girls splashing and calling from their pond. Sometimes the boys try to spy on them but they are usually caught. The girls appear less interested. If they do ever peer from the leaves they are more secret and cleverer. Also, they seem more self-contained than the boys, older; as though in possession of some female wisdom: a mystery reserved to them.

They have drawn lots and Fidus has the shortest straw. He will be the last to dive. He stands a little apart from the other boys. He has friends but he is not one of the heroes, or, for that matter, the buffoons. The rest like him. It is not in his nature to ingratiate himself, nor is it necessary.

At fourteen Fidus has a serviceable body, made not for grace but stamina. Survival. Naked like the rest, he is compact. He will grow another foot but he will never be tall. He has shortish legs and arms but strong muscles and powerful lungs. On the sprint he does not shine but last year he won the marathon, pacing himself, running at first with the pack then coming up from the rear. Only for the last kilometre was he abreast with the leader and overtook to win in the last hundred yards. For his age, he was unusually aware of his strengths and his weaknesses. He ran with his head. And then, accepting the silver chalice presented by the Master of Soldiers in the grounds of the Villa d'Este, Fidus Octavius was just a boy, pleased to win, embarrassed and triumphant, hoping his mother saw. She did.

The boys are naked, except for one, a non-participant. It is the tradition that he should dress as a well-born woman, paint his face and present the wreath to the Victor. As a rule he then gets thrown in himself.

Fidus Octavius shivers although it cannot be cold, even in the shade. It is his turn. He dives, not elegantly, to mocking applause.

Then he opens his eyes to silence. It is wonderful, the green and the gold. From this upper water Fidus can make out the waving shapes of the dumb world above. If the dead could look back through mirrors to the living, they would see something like this: people whose voices cannot be heard, to whom it is impossible to talk. They cannot see you and you cannot join them in their airy world, even though the mirror is not of glass but water.

Fidus kicks his feet and swims deeper.

At the bottom of this pool of legends there is said to be an ancient fish. Older even than the Old Romans, he is the guardian of the spring. The story says that if the fish is ever caught and killed the spring will dry up. But this is a pond of stories. There is another that warns: one day the great fish will swallow all the water in the pool, the world itself.

And in another, he has teeth. If you swim too deep he will bite off your toes and then your feet and then your legs. Finally, he will eat your heart.

Time is different down here. In the other world you hear

clocks, bells, birds, voices that spell out time. Up there you can guess the time of day from the sun.

The diver's lungs are beginning to ache.

But still Fidus swims deeper. He has this idea of seeing the fish, of catching it and holding its scaly flanks between his hands, kicking his way to the surface. It would gasp in the bright sun and then he would let it go.

He closes his eyes, forces himself down and then feels something at his ankle. Fish? Weed? He is only caught for a matter of seconds but that is enough. He kicks free, puffs out a small breath, hears the beating of his own heart in his ears. Fidus opens his eyes and can see nothing. The elements of this water world are utter darkness and breathlessness.

Yet for a moment, he nearly swims on down.

By the time Fidus Octavius surfaces, gasps on the bank and is supported, laughing and choking, to receive the Victor's wreath, he has forgotten that queer impulse to go on. It will come back years later when, on campaign in Africa, a fever brings nightmares in brief blinks of sleep. There is the bottomless pool and the fish, and then the father he has never seen, who is death.

The dream returns whenever he is anxious or exhausted.

He cried out in the night at Tivoli, frightening Livia, so at last he had to tell her. In the marriage bed, in the sheets sweetly stained by their loving, Fidus Octavius woke in tears and sweat.

His eyes had that expression Livia had noticed before: when Octavius, caught unawares, appeared to be looking at something no one else could see.

She kissed his wound.

'Hush. It's all right.'

'It was like being on one side of a mirror and all I had to do was swim through. But I didn't. I wanted to be Victor.'

'I know. I saw you.' Livia smiled against his shoulder.

'But we didn't meet until I was at the Academy. Then I saw you, at the pool.'

'I saw you first, the day you were Victor. Girls are better spies. You never caught us. We were hiding in the ilex leaves. I can't think now why we were interested in naked boys. You stayed under too long. I thought you'd drowned. But let's stop talking or we'll never sleep.'

This was that last late summer before Syria, the abundant autumn of their passion. Octavius felt Livia slide down the bed, her lips at his sex. Then she mounted and rode him and called him again: my horse.

Afterwards, as they lay, fingers entwined, her head on his shoulder, Livia said: 'It was probably Rufus who made you think of the pool.'

'It was only a dream.'

The sulphur in the baths reminds Octavius painfully of the cuts on his face from the grit in the sandstorm. Octavius eases his position and mops his forehead. He reflects on the idiocy of his behaviour in the storm. If an officer had taken such an irresponsible risk he would have reprimanded him.

Going to the edge. That was the way Severus had described his reason for volunteering. It is an urge Octavius recognises.

He says to Severus: 'That boy who nearly drowned in the pool was Rufus. My son.'

'I'm sorry, sir. I didn't know. But he was all right?'

'Oh, yes.'

'I never met him at the Academy.'

'He refused to take his place. Maybe he thought I was angry with him. It was a difficult period. We didn't handle it too well. I suppose many young men find Tivoli restricting.'

'But it was an accident?'

'Probably.

Severus understands that this is not a subject to pursue.

'Where is he now, sir?'

'He joined up. In the ranks. We had no idea until it was done. The Fifth Legion.'

'Africa?'

'That's the last I heard from my wife. Before the mail stopped.'

Sometimes Octavius feels himself awkwardly balanced, living in the present and yet his dumb gaze turned in one direction towards his father, in another, to his son.

Severus hides his anxiety as he glances at the General. That business in the storm. The evening walks in the Valley of Tombs. Hatim's death must have hit him. He has aged lately in some way Severus cannot define.

'Can I ask you something, sir? Have you ever regretted becoming a soldier?'

'Never.' Octavius smiles. 'To be a General, however, is another matter.' He stretches, rubs his neck and pulls the towel around him. 'I had a tutor called Pausonias who used to bash Plato into me, though I never learned Greek properly. Do you remember when the souls of the dead are choosing their next lives? Odysseus is glad to find that of a private and obscure man.'

'That's what you'd have chosen, sir?'

Octavius pulls on his robe, ponders.

'I'll tell you something, Severus. I don't know. I really have no idea.'

Octavius laughs. A bath in the miraculous spring, the company of Severus, have cheered him. They dress and walk together towards Octavius's tent. In a moment the setting sun will reach the Arab castle. In the cooler air the camp is moving more easily. Voices call. Orders are shouted. A Bedouin woman carrying a dead chicken by the neck steps aside as the General passes. The sky is innocent of wind. The desert retreats. Octavius knows these smells so well, better than those of his own hearth: the stench of men, of horse, camel, cooking, sand, sweat drying in the kinder dusk.

'How is our visitor?'

'He'll live but he still can't speak. I hope to get some sense from him tomorrow. His lips were burned black.'

Octavius nods.

'And Probus's mission?'

'The women? Probus seems to know what he's doing.'

'Probus always knows what he's doing.'

'He's not sure the women are the answer. They might even bring trouble.'

The General is still sharp.

'Probus and Otto. I know. They want a foray.'

'Something like that.'

They have arrived at the Temple of Bel. Bel, Octavius wonders. Or Bal – the ancient Bedouin god of water, spring, river, life? That would make sense.

'You remember when you first came, Severus? We dug up the museum. Good days.'

'They were.'

Octavius looks around in wonder, as though he were seeing for the first time.

'This light,' he says.

Those were good times. The digging, often for days finding nothing. And then a treasure. Finding much they did not understand.

Severus had brought books. Those helped. At least, they knew what they were digging for.

Now and then, to get a perspective and for the pleasure of it, Octavius rode Dido, those spring days, around the vast site. There was a fresh green on the trees, some blossom. A low-growing succulent that had looked so uninteresting in winter, flowered a reddish-purple.

Octavius remembered how he had first heard of Palmyra in the school-room. Gaius Germanicus had spoken of the city in the desert as a fine example of old Roman strategy. Control without subjugation. As a free city under Hadrian Tadmor won protection and prosperity, Rome had her outpost against Parthia. A fair exchange.

And then Pausonias's dryness cut into that memory. 'Territory,' he said. 'That's all there is to any empire. Stand back and look at history. It's a disgraceful story of greed and brutality. Think in minutes. Imperial Rome lasted about fifteen. But go to Tadmor. By all means, go. And when you are there, look. You might be surprised.'

Octavius was surprised. As he and Severus stepped down into what had once been the museum and walked around, they found faces that looked back at them with a gaze both human and direct. The jewelled ferocious matron. The old woman, gentle, sad.

And behind many of the figures there was a stone curtain.

Severus held the torch.

'That was the curtain between life and death. Beyond it there is the afterlife. Or perhaps nothing?'

Octavius shivered. He was aware of an intimation; it could have come from future time when he would choose to walk in the Valley of Tombs.

Meanwhile, the air in here was stale. Severus coughed. It was even a little dangerous. Until he could get it shored up, the roof might fall in, there could be scorpions. In a glass case there were two pathetic mummies, one with its lower teeth intact. There was more life in those stone faces.

The General and his lieutenant made their way up into the bright day.

At that time there was still mail delivery. Hope, even, that Livia and Paulina might be allowed to come.

Octavius had written to Livia that spring evening. Although the nights were cold he had already moved into his summer quarters in the Temple of Bel.

'. . . More than ever I want you to come here. I long to show you this place . . . I have no archaeology and Severus little more than a few books, but if we can uncover something! It is not the pomp of Empire that grips me. History a bit, of course. To brush away the dust that has lain on this city since the last excavations so long ago. More though, the feeling I had when I looked into those faces in the museum – so far from our much-admired classical, their eyes are turned east, I think – what I felt was the connection with those people, something to do with common humanity. Perhaps I'm naive but it puts history in its place, somehow.

'With the everyday business here – the building, daily orders, reconnaissance, reports to Tivoli, dealing with the Bedouin, everything, I don't know how much time we'll have but I intend to go on. All kinds of plans. Did I tell you, it's mostly limestone which explains the golden light the stone gives out under the sun?

'I miss you so much, my love. Most of all in ordinary ways, which are the most painful. At this time of day, when we would sit quietly together and talk or not talk, by the hearth, or walk in the garden . . .'

Octavius remembers that letter and those days. The freshness of his excitement. The figure they found the next day close to the shaft down to the museum, of a giant creature like a lion, with a gazelle resting against it, as though in peace. Later Hatim told him the name: Allat. A goddess.

He tries to remember when it was that excitement turned to passion and then in that passion there was an element of frenzy: as if among these ruins and memorials and tombs and fallen houses and broken hearths he were half-expecting to find his own face looking back at him.

He remembers that soon after this letter Livia's correspondence arrived censored. And then at last one of his letters to her was returned, opened, resealed and undelivered.

The sulphur stream of Ain Efqa gushes out from the grotto to run above ground where the Bedouin women beat their fleeces and do their washing. The men are allowed to bathe there in the late afternoon. Since the episode of the soldier and the Bedouin girl and Hatim's outrage, Otto himself, or a guard he can rely on, is posted by the stream. Not for fear of the Bedouin but to keep the men from any girl who might follow a goat or simply wander in that direction.

As he dresses, Octavius can hear their shouts though not their words. He can guess what they are shouting about, why they are livelier than usual. They have heard that the whores are coming.

Octavius still has a sense of well-being. Thanks to Severus and the wonder, briefly recaptured, of that miracle of the light.

He would have liked to write to Livia about the Bedouin and the death of his old friend, their chief, but he must make do with his journal, he must contain Livia in his head, talk to her there.

By the time Octavius has opened the book he locks away every night, his servant appears with a message.

Antarah, the son of Hatim, chief of the Bedouin, asks to speak with the General.

And there is another interruption around midnight. Octavius has fallen asleep, his head on his table, the journal his pillow, when by the light of a dry thunderstorm the salt flats blink and from the direction of Damascus, crowded and complaining in the back of a horse-drawn wagon, the women wake everyone. Dogs bark. Otto runs to meet Probus on the road from the desert. There are shouts from the barracks. Octavius wakes. The whores have arrived.

5

You know me now. I am Livia.

You may have guessed, the people with whom we are hiding in the Tuscan hills are Christians. A secret community, they have lived here for generations, working as farmers. They never advertised their faith and since the Terror, they go to great lengths to conceal it.

In the last few years they have been joined by others like me: a teacher and his wife, an elderly man who was a priest before the Prohibition.

They all have Latin names, naturally, but among themselves several address each other by chosen baptismal names. Such as Matthew who has charge of the sheep and Mary his wife, a pretty woman my own age. She and I have become friends. Our children play together. They are out there now persecuting the cat with too much attention.

I'm sorry. I'm still confused and anxious about our future – about Paulina's future. I should explain that after the Concordia, when the Commonwealth was set up, long ago, the ban on religion must have seemed entirely reasonable. I am trying to be fair. I do understand the argument: that history tells us faith – or rather, the practice of it – brought nothing but strife and dissension, misery, martyrs, fanaticism.

At first, they were not intolerant. The state was strong enough to permit aberrations. Perhaps it is a sign of the decline towards death of this empire that calls itself an organ of the common weal, that anything, any idea which does not conform has become abhorrent, to be outlawed. There is now a monthly list of banned books. History, already strictly edited, is increasingly revised and republished by a new committee controlled by someone close to the centre of power at Tivoli. The chairman is not named but I have my suspicions. Gaius Germanicus grows fat. He has been promoted to the Academy Board of Tutors and granted a country house.

It was he who betrayed us. My fault. I went to him for help after the agents of the Terror had come to the villa.

I am thankful my dear Octavius has seen none of this. I pray we meet again elsewhere for Tivoli today would break his heart.

I have heard that the Military Command would welcome him back in some high post. But he would be astonished to know that some senators too, are said to be plotting for his return. He never thought himself a Villa d'Este man – and perhaps that is the very reason they want him, as a kind of Augustus. A healer and peacemaker, in his case untarnished by politics, who could command the same respect among the people he has from the army.

I wonder, did he ever fully understand my faith? He supported me in Paulina's baptism. Yes, I believe in his own way, Octavius is appalled by the vision of a universe without meaning. Once that icy breach in life, of death, has intervened, says Lucretius, there is no more waking. The only hell is on earth. Life is given on lease. What an irony that the beauty of his words has given the poet a kind of immortality. And between every line you can read his own rage against death.

Octavius had an absurd respect for my mind. If only he knew. He sees me as the *domina*, the Roman matron who can read Greek when he cannot. And I was the one who fell out of reason and into faith because I could not bear the cold.

It is a relief to talk to Mary who was born into Christianity. Like the ancient Copts, she wears the tattoo of the cross at her wrist: the secret sign for which I know she would happily die. Not that we discuss such things. Her faith is like breathing, she is so sure. If Christ were to stroll one evening out of the olive grove, she would not be surprised.

We talk about ordinary things; the children, the plants we collect to dye our wool; our husbands. She is sorry for me that mine is so far away and prays for his life. We have a chapel in the cellar which is reached through a trap-door under the big kitchen table. We sing softly, I believe in God, the Father Almighty. The few sins we have to confess are quickly absolved by Father Jerome. What we feel together in these services is simple happiness.

I am not as strong as Octavius imagines.

When I think about him, he is the gallant one.

I see him in the city in the desert, looking out from those wide eyes. He will be older, tired. But he is alive. If he were not, I would know.

But then I have no idea if Rufus is alive, and he is my flesh.

Mary guesses how afraid I am for them both but she says nothing. It is better not to think. We use no clocks here but measure our days by darkness and light. I have cut off my hair and my hands are rough. I am thankful for the physical labour and grateful for my body. It is strong.

6

Well, they've arrived. Bang on midnight yowling like cats on heat.

Sorry. Otto.

Lieutenant Probus had a time of it getting here. We couldn't spare the fuel so he took a wagon. Nearly lost a wheel by the time he got back. The horses were trying to bolt and you can't blame them if you've ever seen a thunderstorm here. Bolts of lightning seem to fizz up from the desert floor. If it rains you get flash floods.

You can imagine the racket. Dogs, horses, thunder, screeching women. The whole city lit up clear as day.

Then the sky bursts, the rain starts. And we have to get the women under cover. What a sight. Got my face scratched. The idea was to put them in what's left of the new town, outside Zenobia's wall, but overnight the only place was the punishment block near officers' quarters and the Praetorium. Came up with some pitta bread and water and locked the door myself. If I had my way I'd throw away the key.

Sat up with the lieutenant and made sure he had some meat with his bread and beer. Then he told me, he'd got the whores from Homs. That's on the Orontes, on the road to Damascus. He'd made contact through one of the Bedouin, bribed him, that is. The women aren't Bedouin. Most aren't even whores by profession. But the Savages took their men a while back and sacked their town. The women were raped and left. Lieutenant Probus says they're half-starved. They were scratching a living in the ruins. He had to let them bring their children so that's more mouths to feed. It's a bit pathetic really. I've seen some things in my time but pimping's no job for a soldier like Lieutenant Probus.

I don't know how it'll work out. I'm a man like any other. I daresay I'll make use of them. Maybe that way I can get this itch out of my head or my groin, whichever it is. That Bedouin girl in the red skirt, Hatim's daughter, the one that keeps the goats. I don't trust myself there. The way she walks, the straight back, the sway of her thighs, a look as if she's laughing at you. She's hardly more than a child but she knows about Otto. Cunt-struck.

In spite of the broken night Octavius wakes early. This is his favourite time of day in summer, when the sun is just up. He steps outside his tent, the guard salutes and stands aside. Octavius looks. The sun stares back from that easternmost of the old Roman frontiers, the Euphrates.

There is no sign of last night's disturbances. Gazing out over the city he once desired so feverishly to dig, discover, learn, restore, he reflects how this place is like an ocean in its certainty and deafness and vastness. In dumbness it absorbs and forgets all frenzies of the human insect. It is dwarfing and at the same time calming. If death were like this it would be good.

Probus will be here soon to make his report. And Severus, when he has interrogated the stranger. If the stranger lives. And Hatim's son. Then Octavius must be the General.

Meanwhile he is reminded of Africa: the tropic zone, which has the same capacity for putting intruders in their place. There Rufus went. There Octavius stumbled out of the narrow strip of green to find himself on the last beach. If only he could see, there was India. A dhow was pinned on the milky water, waiting for the wind. There was a curl of spume on the coral reef and then the sea was bland again. An old man, a scribble of rags, prostrated himself to face Mecca. An

Arab voice, the muezzin, the call to prayer. Octavius walked back up the beach into the trees. He was younger then. His step was hopeful. The leaves had eyes. He was looking at a footprint in the sand when the blade of the panga felled him.

In those days, Octavius remembers, he had whole continents within his head. Mapped behind his eyes were Africa, Arabia, India. In the short time since his schooldays the Savages had moved further north and west but the Commonwealth was still strong. Her legions maintained and imposed peace, held the frontiers. At that age Octavius never questioned the new Roman ethic. He still believes, this summer morning in Tadmor, that there is honour to power if it brings peace.

And Gaius Germanicus had been right when he said that six months in the army would knock metaphysical anxieties out of Octavius's head. Perhaps that explained why, as a young soldier, he was happy. When your first concern is to obey orders and stay alive, you don't worry much about immortality. He found the immediacies of army life agreeable. He had been trained for this. Only a few years out of the Academy, he looked back on the schoolboy arguing with Gaius Germanicus in the Fiesole garden with a kind of fatherly indulgence.

He did not want to die because Livia had married him a year after their meeting at the pool by the ilex grove. And he wished to live because he relished the ease with which he inhabited his body, its obedience, its simple vigour. He looked up at the night sky of Africa and saw continents, oceans, tides, shoals, that imaged and reflected the worlds within his skull. There was a harmony then between the visible and the dream.

The blade slashed and Octavius was swimming down again, too deep in the bottomless pond at Tivoli. He opens his eyes but he cannot see. His lungs ache. He cannot breathe. There is death. There is his father. There is the great fish who is as old as the world and could swallow the pool and the world and the stars.

Rufus is not yet in the nightmare brought on by fever and the damp airs of the Indian ocean where wounds heal badly. Rufus is not yet born. He is a small fish in Livia's belly.

The fever broke. Octavius's eyes fluttered open. He could not move his head to the right. His skull was empty.

In an unconscious and familiar gesture, Octavius fingers the scar tissue on the right side of his neck. For many years that was the only attention he paid it. Not until he came to Syria did the old wound start to trouble him. It has become difficult to turn his head to the right. There is a dull ache, sometimes a sharp pain, and he is grateful for Severus's oils. It strikes Octavius as an irony that his body in its ageing now remembers a wound he had all but forgotten.

Sounds are very clear at this time of day in still air. From the Temple of Bel Octavius can hear Dido fussing in the stables by Diocletian's camp. He knows her voice. He believes the mare is conscious of her status. She knows that she was chosen by Hatim and is favoured by Octavius. She is arrogant among the other horses, has a way of carrying her head, arching her neck, quick-stepping on high hooves, as though she were neither horse nor man but queen of a country no one else could see. She permits only Octavius to ride her and then she is not exactly ridden. She and her master become one horse-man-creature.

Octavius would like to ride now but the General has work to do. He wonders if the stranger lives and if he does, what will Severus have to report from his interrogation. He is aware that he himself should have gone to see the man.

Could the truth be that Octavius is not sure he wants to hear what the stranger might have to say? Perhaps he fears the breaking of the silence.

It was almost a year after their arrival that Hatim made Octavius the gift of Dido.

In that time Octavius had walked out to the Bedouin camp at least once a week when his day's duties were done. He went at first for pragmatic reasons. The men were suspicious of the Bedouin. It was important that the General should set an example. Besides, there was barter to be agreed. And Octavius had to judge for himself whether or not the nomads could be trusted.

Quite soon, he went for pleasure as well as business: always careful to respect the chief's dignity. In winter Octavius caught fleas from the goatskin tent. He was thankful when the weather grew warm enough for the two of them to sit outside by the fire.

This was before Probus arrived and Octavius wonders now, in what language did we speak? I had a few words of Arabic from our time in Egypt and the northern Arabia campaign at Azraq and Keraq; Hatim a little French and English. We managed.

I can see it now behind my eyes and smell it. At the edge of the loom of light from the dung fire figures move like the shadows of reality in Plato's cave. Sometime later I mentioned this and so we came to discuss philosophy (I heard Pausonias laugh).

First though, the fire is like a family hearth. The Bedouin are no longer the wanderers they were. The Savages have put an end to a nomad life that was already declining. But this fire reminds me; I have thought before how inimical the desert is to us; and yet to these people it is quite another landscape, as familiar to them as our villas and our gardens and fields are to us. They could chart every well and spring, every bad and good place. Stones arranged flatly or in cairns mark beds, act as signposts, tell stories. The place is full of voices. Scratchings in a stone cleft I was shown between Keraq and the Red Sea, of a man and a woman and a beast and a god, are signals from a time older than any of the temples or the cathedrals of our ancients. For the tribes these dangerous sands and stretches of bleak basalt are their city. The air is full of voices.

So we would eat with our fingers around the fire from a dish passed round among the men. The women served us and took their own food apart. Not that there is anything servile about Bedouin wives and daughters. They are noisy, ready with laughter and temper. Their black hair shines with grease or oil. When there is a celebration, they dye their hands and faces with henna. In the evenings they embroider with the smallest stitches and weave bright rugs. Times have been hard since the Savages restricted travel and cut off the Bedouin from their markets in Damascus and further. I bought rugs for my tent and a few of the flexible screens they use to support the walls of their tents against the wind. Also a blanket of warm fleece and two woollen cloaks dyed with indigo. I said to Livia in a letter, the colour is too close to the old imperial purple for my taste.

I had met the child Manah that first spring by the stream and looked out for her on my evening visits. Sometimes she detached herself from the flickering figures moving around the fire and I would find her standing at my shoulder. But then Hatim would clap and order her away.

His voice was hoarse. He had bright eyes and a thin, mobile face. I thought of him as old but he had probably looked much the same for twenty years. His narrow hands were eloquent. They cut and slashed and implored and in pleasure or laughter he would raise them, fingers fluttering. He had a long scar from his eye to his chin.

I smiled at Manah.

I said: ‘I have a daughter, too.’

‘And sons?’

'Yes. A son.'

'Good. A son is best. I have two sons. Imru is a fool. Perhaps Antarah is better.'

There would be silences.

Then Hatim said: 'The Romans are here before. There are stories. They went away.'

He nodded.

Another time, as we drank yet another glass of scalding tea, he asked: 'You have gods?'

'No. My wife has a god.'

'What is his name?'

'Jesus.'

Hatim nodded again as though I had spoken of an old acquaintance.

'Yes. Isa.'

I shifted from one haunch to the other. The fire smoked. An unseen camel complained, the wind was coming up.

Then the flame was clean again and by its light I drew in the sand with my knife the carvings I had seen in Wadi Rum.

'Nabatean? Nabat?'

'I have seen. Many gods.'

Was Hatim bored? Tired? This was before Probus and Severus arrived but Otto was there from the start. I guessed that against orders he would have followed me. He would be waiting with a patience peculiar to him, somewhere in the dark not far away. On my orders we had stored our modern weapons in the armoury but Otto would have his hand on the narrow blade I had seen him honing. He would be surprisingly quick on his short legs. He would have the steel in through the ribs and up.

Even without a knife Otto knows the exact point at which to strike a man to kill with the side of his hand. Not that any one man alone would have stood a chance against the Bedouin. Otto must have been aware of this. But his fidelity is amazingly dogged. I know he keeps an eye on me when I walk at dusk in the Valley of Tombs. I am astonished by such persistent faithfulness, beyond the bounds of duty. It seems to me that in my age I have wandered far into solitude, close to madness, away from the General's right to command obedience. I know Otto would die for me but I cannot think why.

In those days though, I was not acquainted with such doubts. This was before the silence and the strict shadows of the tower tombs.

In the middle of my life youth had come upon me again. I was full of plans and questions and yet had the use of prudence. I was no longer the fool who was so dazzled by the Indian Ocean he did not see the blade of the panga. I could talk with Hatim.

The chief examined intently my scratchings in the sand and seemed to recognise them. He said, as a boy he had been to that place, when the tribes still wandered. He had been as far as the Hejaz, to Mecca, in the lands that are now a part of Arabia Perdita. Later, I learned he had got the scar on his face from the Savages, in those countries. I had hopes of intelligence concerning the Savages but I could tell, at that time anyway, he was reluctant to speak of them

Instead Hatim began to talk about his people's old faith. His tone was conversational, as though he were discussing family or friends.

He spoke of a moon-god and a sun-god, sacred caves and springs and a holy palm tree to which tribute was made of weapons, garments and rags. He lowered his voice and his fingers fluttered when he told me about the jinn, the demons of the desert. In one breath he spoke of Allah and of Venus, the morning star.

'They say in the south the Savages make human sacrifice to this good lady. It was so before and is again.'

'Do you believe in these gods?'

Hatim shrugged.

'My people need them.'

The fire died down. I looked up. The stars that had been

dimmed by the flame were brilliant again. Hatim followed my gaze.

I mentioned Plato and the souls in the cave.

'Sometimes I think we are chained like that. That is how I feel when I look up.'

'We know this philosopher. We had a wise man, Al-Farabi, who explained his words to us. He died in Damas. There were others.'

There were not enough words between us to talk any more about gods or philosophers. And in the breeze, rising again, I heard Pausonias. So the dog-soldier is speaking of philosophy?

I thought of all that had been discovered. The creation of the universe and its likely end had been explained long ago. Gaius Germanicus had taught us that mystery had been driven like a malevolent hag from the earth. The chalk scratched. He wrote on the board: THERE IS NO QUESTION THAT CANNOT BE ANSWERED.

I remembered the complacent relish with which he made us transcribe Horace's words about Venus fled and Lyce preserved as an aged crow for young men to study, laughing, while the torch burned out and collapsed in ashes: a pathetic successor to Cynara, who might have been a real woman, who was loved and died. Even then, bored, restless to get out of the school-room, I had the feeling that the poet's apparent brutality veiled a pain Gaius Germanicus would never understand, even if he lived for ever. Any more than he could grasp the anguish and longing, the difficult questions, that drove Pausonias to open his veins and not to call out as his blood coloured the water pink.

The fire had collapsed into itself.

Hatim said: 'If you look too long into a fire you cannot see the stars.'

Now we could. I pointed and Hatim nodded. There was Venus, dead perhaps in the light-years it took for her picture to reach us, but brilliant still in that celestial graveyard.

Otto would be waiting. I might have overstayed my welcome. The figures around the fire had long gone. I shuddered. It was cold. My arms were empty for Paulina but I must not embrace Manah. She was a child. Perhaps I could bring her presents? I wondered if she still had the tin eagle I gave her that first spring by the sacred stream.

I stood. In clumsy Arabic I wished Hatim that the morning would find him well.

The breeze had settled into a wind. It snatched at the ashes of the fire and they whirled all around us, spiralling up; then fell at our feet, cold and dead, and the desert took them back.

In spite of the many difficulties, I think Hatim and I became true friends. Strangely, I felt we were closer before Probus arrived and was able to translate for us. To have an interpreter between us made communication at the same time easier but more formal.

Now I look back on it, it was an improbable friendship. After all, I was the occupying General. And, as Livia has observed over the years, I am a shy man. It was not repugnance alone that kept me from the court around the Villa d'Este. Quite simply, I have never been at ease in social gatherings of any kind. It is as though I had never learned the language.

In that bronze bust Livia insisted that I sit for in Alexandria I did not recognise myself. I saw myself as a plain soldier, best doing his job, awkward in company. This was a man with a strange gaze. Except with Livia and a few friends – and now and then with Severus in spite of the difference in rank – I have felt not so much shy as set at a slight distance from the ordinary world. When I thought about it I measured those few paces into the noisy room of life but something stopped me from taking them, as though my feet too were cast in bronze.

Livia came out to meet me. She took my hand and I

followed. But Rufus turned away and I never saw him again.

In the early days of my visits to Hatim I looked at Manah and decided it would have been easier with a daughter, to take those few paces, to hold her in my arms.

I remember Hatim rarely came to see me in the camp. It is the custom to return hospitality but I did not press the matter. Instead, before our supply line was cut off, I took such gifts as I could find: beads and combs Livia sent, provisions, a buckle, a belt, a saddle.

Hatim came twice to the camp. Once, when they caught a soldier with one of the Bedouin girls in a Tower Tomb. That was later, in the period when fraternisation was permitted: the only time I remember Probus giving bad advice.

Before, a year after our arrival, Hatim sent a messenger to ask if the General would receive him. Then, in the early evening, before the cold night of early autumn, we saw a procession coming towards us from the Bedouin settlement. I stood. I had lost my second-in-command on a desert patrol but the faithful Otto was close. Under his cloak he probably had his hand on his knife. I know he disapproved of my ruling that before the Bedouin only the guards could carry arms.

Hatim led, mounted on a camel, as were his young sons, Antarah and Imru. Antarah appeared to be leading a horse. Other Bedouin followed on camels or on foot, with a company of their women bringing up the rear.

Hatim dismounted. We exchanged formal greetings and then he embraced me, brushing my cheek with his, twice. Then he called out in Bedouin. The boy Antarah slid off his camel and stepped forward, leading a young white mare who did not want to be led. She snorted, high-stepped sideways, tossed her head. The women let out that extraordinary labial ululation reserved for celebration. I guessed it was they who had decked out the horse like a bride. She wore no saddle and in place of reins a rope of flowers and leaves, with a kind of breast-plate of gold coin necklaces and sequins. A rich silky cloth was flung over her back.

Hatim opened his hands wide, palms upwards. He meant: she is yours.

His gravity of ceremony cracked. He smiled. His fingers danced.

'No name,' he said.

'Too great a gift,' I answered. But I was smiling too.

I took a pace forward and laid a hand on her neck. She was trying to throw off the flowers. I spoke. She seemed to listen.

On that occasion Hatim sat for a while on a rug outside my tent. Otto managed to hide his suspicions, made a fire, brought coffee, pitta bread, water and dates. The chief dismissed everyone but his two boys, who waited for him by the camels. I could smell Otto's doubt. The boys were probably just as uneasy in the camp of the strangers.

But Hatim and I were happy that night. We talked a little, of horses and the city, crops and weather. I think we discussed magic and I asked him about astrology but could not understand his answer.

There was a friendly silence. Hatim let out a deep sigh. There was a promise in the air of the first frost.

I can't remember why I mentioned the Savages but I can never forget how Hatim replied.

He gestured towards the desert and put his hand to his own breast and then to mine. He shrugged.

He meant: we are all Savages.

I went to see the stabled mare and named her Dido for Livia and our agreed signal: that when Paulina had been baptised Livia would write of Virgil. And I recalled from the school-room that Dido had called her secret love for Aeneas, marriage.

I miss you, Hatim. Your silences, the understanding between us; I see you riding away flanked by your boys. And passing between the lights by the guardposts, without turning you raise one hand in farewell. And then you are gone beyond the palm-grove into the desert. Darkness has fallen, cold pitch. Winter comes.

* * *

Probus makes his report to the General. He looks dead on his feet. He says the whores and their children are being moved to the ruins of the new city beyond the wall.

Octavius is sitting behind his camp-table, inside his tent.

'I'm sorry you had to take this on, Probus.'

'Sir.'

Octavius fingers his scar.

'We can't have you minder to a brothel. You'd better put Otto in charge. We'll make the new city out of bounds except at scheduled times.'

'I've posted the order, sir.' Probus looks embarrassed. 'Otto's working out visiting hours, so to speak. For the men and officers – different days, of course.'

'Of course.' Even at ease, stocky Probus always seems to be standing to attention. Octavius leans back in his chair. He surveys his lieutenant. 'You're not sure this is the answer, are you, Probus?'

'There are risks.'

Octavius nods.

'I can't risk a foray, you must know that. We've never had aerial reconnaissance. We can't even get reports from Tivoli. I suppose, a small intelligence-gathering expedition? I'll give it some thought.'

'I speak Arabic, sir. I can ride a camel. If we can get one of the Bedouin as guide.'

'Perhaps.'

'The men believe we're being watched.'

'We probably are. Get some rest, lieutenant. I'll inspect the guard at noon.'

Octavius's servant brings his breakfast. Afterwards, he stays inside his tent. He hears shouts and whistles, the noise of wagon-wheels. The whores are being taken to the new city. Today perhaps Antarah will come.

The General has not given anyone the word that has been

in his head like a stone since Hatim's death. He cannot fathom the connection between the word and the loss of his old friend, but there is one.

The day after Hatim died Octavius wrote in his journal.

Retreat. I cannot speak of this to anyone although I am tempted to discuss it with Severus. I must resist that temptation because it is my decision alone and a heavy one.

Livia, if I could speak to you I would say that I no longer see any point in our presence here. Tadmor has become a useless outpost of a silent empire.

I love this place. It engages my soul in a way I could never explain, even to you. But strategically it is of no significance. The mountain at our backs is the natural border, so far as any frontier is natural. Sometimes I think that all this business of men and the maps they make, the lines they draw upon the earth, has no more substance than a mirage.

At this time of year, midsummer, we have seen oceans at noon, armies advancing from an empty plain, the brave flash of steel, banners fluttering in still air. And cities of windows and towers mock us from the salt-flats, shimmer and dissolve.

That night the storm returns. Antarah does not come. Otto reports that the women are settled in the new city. He has provisioned them from the garrison's own shrinking stores, bartered with the Bedouin for a few hens together with fleeces and other necessities. These are country women, who have lived for a long time houseless without husbands; I suppose we have saved them. I can only hope that Probus is wrong in his forebodings. He fears trouble. My anxiety is self-indulgent. I wonder, however desperate they are, what right do we have to use these women as whores?

I am writing this in the small hours of the night because I must put down what Catus, the stranger, said. In any case, I could not sleep, the storm is too noisy. It is wonderful too.

Severus took me to the cell after dark. He said the man

would speak to no one but me. The cell was clean. They had washed him but there was still a smell I recognised: fear, faeces, sweat.

I knelt down. I have seen deaths in battle but oddly none in peace. I took the thin hand in mine.

'What is your name?'

'Catus.'

'Where are you from?'

'Tivoli. The Senate.'

'Wet his lips.'

'He can't swallow.'

'Put a wet cloth to his lips.'

Severus was scared, I could tell. He does not know about the darkening of the eyes before death. He does not know death.

What Catus had to tell me, between rattling breaths, was a terrible story.

Tivoli is in turmoil. The Commander of the empire, Lucius Tarquinius, has declared himself Emperor. The dissenters in the Senate have joined with those of the same mind in the Military Command. There are few who dare oppose the Villa d'Este. News from the frontiers is confused. In the city there are fires every night, riots, looting, martial law. Lucius Tarquinius has issued an order for my execution.

Catus made his dangerous journey to bring a message I can hardly credit and don't wish to hear.

They want me to return with the Legion and to put on the purple. They offer me the greatest name of all: Augustus.

Is this what you meant, Pausonias, by the difficult questions? I doubt it. You had no time for affairs of state, empires, emperors, courtiers, kings.

You said Plato had the last word on the subject of human vainglory. For him one year was a thousand and a thousand one. So if there is life everlasting we shall return to what we were, no more, no less. The bee fretting against the window. Your wisdom, your weariness. What you said in your way of leaving, was that human life is a tragedy. The best we dog-soldiers can do is to endure and to leave it with grace.

This is a dry storm. No rain will fall. I step outside my tent and look out as a lightning flash summons the city to life. I hear the voices of merchants in the agora. I see the dead awaken in the Valley of Tombs and walk out from their towers, stiff with eternity; bewildered, then laughing, smiling, as they recognise the friends and children they have lost, and turn to embrace.

7

Trouble already. The men smuggled one of the whores into the barracks. Drunk, and they got her drunk. These women have never tasted liquor before. Against their faith. But then so is prostitution and they've taken to that like ducks to water. Not that they had any choice, poor bitches.

So a dozen of them are having a go, taking turns, and Flaminius comes in screeching and goes for her. Guess who has to sort that one out. Yours faithfully, Otto.

I've found one for myself. Nayra. She's older, a sensible sort of woman. No beauty, but it's the young and pretty ones that give the trouble. A cunt's a cunt and she doesn't talk.

I've got them beads and shawls and all sorts of rubbish from the Bedouin. You ought to see them: hardly more than skeletons and all decked out like birds of paradise, gold earrings, henna on their cheeks, fighting over a bit of coloured glass.

They've lived like animals for so long they've probably forgotten what they used to be.

I've been thinking a bit about this. Always used to say, a tart's a tart. But these were wives and mothers and daughters. Men depraved them. Savages first, then others, then us. It's the children I'm sorry for, all covered with sores, their eyes sunk and big. I try to bring them a bit extra. I try not to think what will become of them if we go or if the Savages come.

Since the night the stranger died there have been rumours. The favourite is, there's an army on its way from Tivoli. Only Lieutenant Severus knows the truth and he's not talking, except maybe to the General.

It's evening now, for which my grateful thanks. In the middle of the day the heat here is enough to drive you mad.

Shan't get to Nayra tonight. I'm on watch. There goes the General on his evening walk into the Valley of Tombs. I've brewed up tea and lit the fire but the last few nights he hasn't paused for his usual chat. Wonder what he sees there, what he's looking for?

You get a good view from up here. Sometimes beyond the city and the oasis and the Bedouin settlement, on the horizon, I think I can see stick figures out there where night begins. Savages.

Octavius began to walk in the Valley of Tombs when a letter to Livia was returned, opened and resealed, and then Tivoli fell silent.

Around that time he wrote in his journal.

Livia. This is the only way I can talk to you. Even though you cannot hear me, to speak, even like this, brings you a little nearer.

The silence must end. I shall see you again. Meanwhile I have taken to walking at dusk in the Valley. Among those tower tombs I find some kind of comfort I do not understand. And last night I heard your voice, so clearly. You cried out in the garden at Aswan by the Nile and Rufus was born the next morning. We thought that was the pinnacle of our happiness and perhaps it was. But we were so young, it was easy not to believe in death, or to imagine that we had defeated it. We had both survived wounds – yours in childbirth, mine in Africa. We didn't know that the best was to come in autumn in Tivoli in tangled sheets, with the dish of figs on the floor. You reached for one to feed me and we had the juice on both our mouths; it spurted on your breasts, ample, full of time. The plenitude of a long marriage is richer even than birth.

I am a simple man. Didn't I bore you? Your quick mind always ran ahead of me. I plodded after. Then so wonderfully in our late years, you turned and touched my face and took my hand.

I never spoke like this, did I? My love was dumb. In this place I have found the words that were locked in for so long. At last I have learned to speak and to listen, for there are all kinds of company here, in the wind, in the sand, in the stones. I can tell that Otto does not approve of my solitary walks at dusk. But I am not mad. It is more as though I were awakening into my senses.

Don't worry. I'm still a soldier, Commander of the garrison, aware that if we are truly cut off from Tivoli I must keep the men busy. To that end I am planning to set them to work on the restoration of the Temple of the Signa, within which there was the Holy of Holies. Here the old Romans would lead a recruit to take his oath among the standards of the empire, by the dim light of lamps in that central darkness. Perhaps it's a foolish idea but Severus is enthusiastic. His coming has added so much to life here. I see my youth in both of them, Probus and Severus.

In appearance Severus reminds me of Rufus. I didn't have the words for him, did I? That thought is a hard one I have to live with. I remember, you and I quarrelled when he refused to go to the Academy. I can hear you crying in our bedroom when they brought him back from the pond by the temple ruin. Our son had tried to drown himself and I turned away. I had no words. I sent him to the farm. You were angry and he was hurt. The day he left he imagined I had not forgiven him when the truth was, I should have asked his forgiveness. He answered my silence when he enlisted in the ranks. I passed onto my son my inheritance from my father: the silence of the grave.

But Egypt was good, wasn't it? The river and the desert, that narrow strip of verdant life. I remember you in the garden at Aswan with Rufus in your arms, the hoopoe bird on the lawn. You are young, standing by the purple fall of flowers, waiting for me. You call out but I cannot hear what you are saying.

That was years ago. Since then, in the course of sleepless nights, in the middle of the day's affairs, riding Dido, talking to Hatim or Severus, on his solitary walks, words unasked-for have entered Octavius's head. One of these words is redemption. He can taste it. He wonders if he will ever know what it means.

The General sends for Severus to ride with him. The lieutenant is a good horseman. Better than Probus, or, rather, more graceful. Stocky Probus has great powers of endurance, no horse ever gets the better of him but the sport he was built for is wrestling. The men respect him for this. He has trained them and organises weekly competitions. No one has ever managed to fell him. In the field, he excels at hand-to-hand combat. The men, like Otto, understand Probus. They see Severus as air to Probus's earth, girlish. He is the only officer, apart from the General, not to have used the whores. He has never seen action.

Severus rides lightly. His grey mare hardly feels his weight. Keeping pace with the General, he reins her in at the edge of the oasis where the desert begins. He is the kind of young man you would normally find around the court at the Villa d'Este: someone born to privilege. At his level of society, the sexual ambivalence suggested by those slanting, dark eyes, the full mouth on the edge of a smile, would have done Severus no harm. But Severus chose to come to Tadmor, to go to the edge, the frontier.

Both the General and his lieutenant wear the Arab headdress, the kiffayah, and light cloaks for summer.

Dido dances as she stands. She arches her head away from

the other horse's muzzle. She is no longer young.

Severus's face was a little soft when he first arrived. It is thinner now, the strong nose more evident, the planes of his features sharper, but he does not burn in the sun, his olive complexion simply deepens.

The General looks out to the desert like a sailor in the bows of his ship.

'You heard what Catus had to say?'

'Sir.'

The General smiles.

'And what is your opinion, lieutenant?'

'I have no opinion, sir.'

'I don't believe that.'

'My father never trusted Lucius Tarquinius.'

Octavius nods. Severus has the feeling that the General is laughing at him.

'I was at school with him. He was Gaius Germanicus's favourite.'

A camel walks by, absurdly haughty. Dido snorts.

The high summer sun sucks the colour from everything. Gold drains from the pillars of the city. The sky is white. The sands appear as an ocean.

Octavius says: 'I'm a soldier, no more, no less. I'll tell you, Severus, I had been considering retreat to the mountains.'

He leads the way at a gentle trot.

This is the time of day when the camp falls silent. Even the Bedouin do not move. In the shaking light the horses appear to shudder.

Severus follows the General. He tries to imagine the utter loneliness of this Command. He sees it in the set of Octavius's shoulders. Since the messenger came from Tivoli the General has not, until this morning, called for Severus to ride or to go to the baths, to swim or to talk.

'Severus, you've studied a great deal more history than I.'

'So far as I could, sir. Most of what we were taught was propaganda. When you come down to it, history is simply the chronicle of the fall of empires. It's an inevitable process. And empire is another word for conquest and occupation. Some were patently wicked. Others, benevolent in their way.'

The General has led the way to the open stream.

'And the old Roman virtue? The Golden Age?'

Severus pauses before answering and glances at the General. Octavius has reined in Dido.

'I don't believe governments are capable of moral action. The Pax Romana was a pragmatic exercise, to the benefit of Rome.'

Octavius turns his head.

'So who is capable of goodness?'

'The individual?'

'Ah, yes. I remember now. Plato's philosopher kings. My old tutor, Pausonias. Not that he thought much of that proposition. In his view the philosopher in government would be immediately corrupted.'

The General has dismounted. They lead their horses to drink.

'You know what is on my mind, Severus?'

The lieutenant nods. Standing in the stream, Dido jostles the other mare, tosses her head, flings out spray.

Octavius says calmly: 'I could not perform any act I cannot imagine. Do you understand that, Severus?'

'I think so, sir.'

Severus takes this to mean that they may never go home.

The whole landscape is tranced in heat. Octavius sits in his tent, the map spread open before him. Probus, having the language, has interrogated the women and a clearer picture of the Savages emerges. They take territory but they do not necessarily fortify or hold it. They left Damascus a dead city, Homs too and Hama. They are at Dayr az Zawr on the Euphrates and in the land between the mountains and the sea that was once the Lebanon, once a part of greater Syria.

Probus is disinclined to give credit to the women's stories. They have endured such horrors. They weep when they talk, clutch your hand, tell of giants who sweep in on the yellow wind and carry the men away, rape the women, calling all the time on the name of Allah, though they know nothing of any true god. They kill the land. They leave behind them dead crops, poisoned wells. One woman has gone mad with all she has suffered. She squats in a corner, pulls her veil across her face, will not speak or eat or move.

These women believe that Allah will punish them for living after they lost their virtue. They will know torment in the grave. Some cry piteously to be taken to Mecca to atone.

Antarah, the son of Hatim, is coming to the General's tent.

Flaminius is sick. He imagines that the women have brought this illness upon him. They have given him the evil eye. He has a high fever but does not report to the medical officer. Sunstroke is classed as a self-inflicted injury. You can be put on a charge. But this is not sunstroke. Now he has no lovers he languishes, the flesh falls from him. He begs for hashish. Out of habit or inclination a few still come to him but most laugh at him. A couple of drunks beat him up. He makes a scene when one of the whores is smuggled into the barracks. In powder and paint, his dusty finery, Flaminius droops and sulks.

So you see, Livia, there is nothing new under the stars. Inexorably, history repeats herself and all one man can do is to recognise the moment she is on the move again. The only effect she can have on him is to make his life more or less comfortable, shorter or longer. Our true life is contained within an area no wider than the circle of light from Hatim's fire. In that small arena we have to do the best we can. I mean, to live with ourselves and each other.

I tend to agree with Lucretius that there is no spirit beyond death. But, I begin to think, we have to live as though we had immortal souls, as if in all of us there is a flame that cannot be put out. And we are all guardians of our own flame.

Your Christians believe that. It is more difficult for the rest of us.

We hear there is a Roman Emperor once more. The news made me think of those cosmologists who taught that time at a certain point of light will begin to run backwards. Everything must be enacted again. Lucius Tarquinius, Commander of the empire, has declared himself Emperor. You remember our compulsory attendances at the Villa d'Este? The courtiers, the sycophants? We should have realised: in his imagination Lucius Tarquinius was already Emperor. I recall you couldn't abide his bad breath.

I wonder if he realises of what a small pond he is king. Empires, like stars, decay. As the years here pile up I have come to understand that. Sometimes I think I can hear their voices: Greeks, Romans, Zenobia the Palmyrene, Moslems, Germans, and again the Romans. You know they named the outpost on the Euphrates after Alexander's birthplace: Doura Europos? And now Tadmor is a ghost city again, populated by an exhausted garrison and a few Bedouin. If the Savages don't take it – or even if they do – it will fall asleep again. The sands will sweep in and dust its golden pillars, fill our excavations and graves, pile up against the Towers of the Dead. Then a caravan at the source of Efqa or a new conqueror may hear our thin voices on the wind.

I can't explain what has happened to me here, why I hear and see such things. I would have said – and you would agree – I'm not a man given to fancies. My imagination is limited.

And can you imagine me as Augustus? An absurd idea. There will be no age of gold. We have nearly run our course. My duty lies here, surely? I swore allegiance not to an Emperor nor even to a Commander, but to the empire. Until the news came I had been considering retreat, at least to the mountains. As things are now, my place is to hold this frontier. My inclination too.

Except that I am even more afraid for you. Poor Catus died before I could ask him. I suspect and hope you left Tivoli long ago. You are brave but rasher than I. Please take care. You know, sometimes I used to feel dull next to you. You are so quick. I am heavy, prudent. But now you might be surprised. This place has turned me into a star-gazer. Have I told you, the night sky here is of a particular beauty and brilliance? On the edge of the desert, alone or with Severus, I feel humbled, because unlike the old Romans, we know that ours is only one small galaxy in a universe greater than we can imagine. Very soon there comes a point where even the cosmologists can see no further, like a man who leaves the lights of a town behind him and steps into a dark lane.

And there is rapture too, like the folly of the deep.

If he dared Otto would cluck like a mother. Severus too is worried about me, I think. There is no need. For a while I was anxious, considering retreat. But the General is not mad.

My darling Livia, there is one extraordinary thing. I used to think that if you were dead, I would know it. Lately, I have become certain that you are alive. I can hear you speaking! Your voice is muffled and I cannot yet make out what you are saying, but I shall. I repeat, I am not out of my mind. Quite simply I woke in the night to the smell of your skin. Your taste was on my lips. You are very close.

Among his books, Severus has a Bible. He recommends it to me for literary reasons. It is the ancient version before they changed the words. I am beginning to read it, to try to understand your Christianity. So far, it strikes me as beautiful but barbaric. I prefer the story of Odysseus, perhaps because I understand him: why he rejected immortality with Calypso and returned to mortal Penelope. He wanted to go home.

It's midnight. I can hear the guard changing for the nightwatch.

Like an old man I have begun to consider the errors of my

life. They are not many but they are painful. I can't expunge them, wipe away your tears for Rufus, my mother's for my father; and I can't envisage yet how I could redeem myself. You never expected to hear me talk like this, did you?

I have decided to move my winter quarters from Diocletian's camp to the Arab castle with its view of the valley.

From my tent I can see the castle and on the same hill, the great cross. How strange that it should be for us a sign of the worst punishment permitted by army orders; for you a symbol of redemption.

Goodnight, Livia. Don't cry. Sleep. I kiss your eyes.

The men watch the General. They want to know what Catus said. Only their daily tasks, the heat and the whores, keep them from dangerous speculation. Even so, the rumours multiply. The guards who saw the stranger swear he wore a senator's ring on the third finger of his right hand. It is said that he was bringing back-pay from Tivoli and was robbed by Savages. He was a spy. He was a wandering lunatic.

But the most popular story is still that he was a messenger from Tivoli with news that the garrison is to be relieved.

In the hallucinatory light of midsummer they imagine they can see the advance guard of the relieving forces in the foothills, or approaching through the desert. They hear voices.

They watch the General for signs. Normally, at his daily inspection, he makes a point of speaking to the men individually. For a few days there is no inspection and when he does show himself his manner is abstracted. He looks as if he has things on his mind.

At the beginning the men used to talk a lot about home. Not so much after the mail stopped and now not at all, though the arrival of the stranger set some of them thinking. If it weren't for the heat there are a few who might consider making a run for home, if there is no relief.

Otto tells them: the General would have said if there were a legion on its way. Whatever happened is the General's business. He's never let them down.

In any case, the heat brings apathy and sickness. They wait for cool evening to go to the whores in the mud-brick houses of the new city. The women, hashish, beer and a swim in the stream are their only pleasures. Otto keeps up daily drill but there is an outbreak of dysentery. The latrines stink. Men faint on parade. Flaminius keeps them awake at night, raving in delirium. Even hashish won't shut him up. Desert sores are always worst at this time of year. After all these years medical supplies are low. The surgeon has run out of iodine and sulphur powder. They get some stuff from the Bedouin that helps. The sore is a kind of ulcer. It suppurates, greenish, and leaves a white scar.

The heat breeds fantasies. Although there is nothing new about dysentery or sores, the story goes round that the Bedouin or the Savages have poisoned the stream.

With a few words of Arabic among them and a few of French, they have got stories from the whores about the Savages. The women say that they paint themselves with a blue dye, probably indigo. So they are known as the Blue Warriors.

The women are a comfort, and not just for the obvious reason. They may be whores but there is more than one man who sleeps after sex and wakes confused, imagining that he can hear the voice of a girl he once had, or a wife, or a mother, a child calling out in the night; and for that vague second between sleeping and waking, he is at home.

Probus has been waiting. At last the General sends for him.

'So what is your opinion, lieutenant?'

'We'd have no chance, sir, with a few hundred men.'

'I'm afraid you're right, Probus. It seems we must stick it out here until things change. If they change.' Octavius smiles.

He pushes something the size of a large coin across his table.

'Do you know what that is?'

'A seal?'

Octavius nods.

'A seal of office struck secretly by the dissidents. Catus put it in my hand just before he died. I suppose this makes me Emperor in exile, if I choose to crown myself. The head flatters me. We have all aged.'

He puts the seal back in the drawer.

'You and I, Probus, we'd be happy to dodge history, I think. But it seems to have caught us out.' Octavius motions for Probus to sit down. He calls for water. When it comes he empties his glass at once and fills it again. 'Perhaps the worst curse you can put on a man is to oblige him to relive history. By the same token Lucius Tarquinius will not last for ever.' Probus thinks that the General looks weary but calm. 'Were you ever at Keraq, Probus?'

'Yes, sir. The second campaign.'

'So was I. The first. What did they call it? Stemming the barbarian tide. Well, we did that for a bit, didn't we? I wonder why we white faces are so attached to deserts? They're filthy places to fight. You must tell Otto, the men with sores may have the use of the sulphur baths, once a day.'

'What do we tell the men, sir?'

'What do you recommend, lieutenant?'

'The truth, or part of it, I'd say, sir. That is, our posting here has been extended. We hope to restore communications with Tivoli. Meanwhile you are planning autumn manoeuvres.'

The General nods.

'I thought much the same thing.' Octavius eases his neck with his hand. Probus takes himself as dismissed but the General speaks again, in the tone of an afterthought.

'Probus, have you ever seen the Savages?'

'No, sir. I don't know anyone who has, except for the women. They say all kinds of things, of course, most of it not to be relied on. They call them the Blue Warriors.'

'You know what I think, lieutenant? Sometimes I think we've made them up.'

Hatim's son, Antarah, comes to the camp that night with his brother Imru. He rides in at sunset, on horseback. Aware of the courtesies, the General walks out to meet him. For a second, seeing the boy come out of the darkness into the setting sun, he is reminded of Hatim. Antarah has the same thin frame; when he slips from his horse and walks to greet the General, Octavius sees the old chief's narrow hands and head, his way of bearing himself.

'You are welcome.'

Long ago, when his older son was a boy, Hatim had told Octavius that he was named after a great Bedouin hero and poet. His second son, Imru also; though in speaking that name, Hatim sliced the air with his hand. He will make nothing. He is rubbish.

Octavius has had a carpet spread outside his tent, with Bedouin cushions. After greetings, he and Antarah sit. For the moment Probus stands behind Octavius, Imru takes a cushion a little way from his brother. As a child, Octavius recalls, Imru had a dimpled charm. He was the women's favourite. They indulged him while Antarah was always at his father's heels. Imru has grown into fat. He is not yet twenty but has a wife and children. Probus says that Imru is known for his laziness. But then Antarah was so clearly favoured by Hatim, Imru never stood a chance. He must have felt their mother's death, years ago, more sharply than Antarah. He sleeps out his hashish days and appears generally amiable, though vain and lazy. While Antarah sits stiff-backed, Imru lolls on one elbow. Probus judges that he is not entirely to be trusted.

Although he is only two years older, Antarah has inherited or learned to emulate some of his father's dignity. His air is so grave Octavius has to put on extra severity himself when his urge is to smile. It strikes him with shock that Rufus must be the same age.

After the ceremony of formal greeting, Antarah presents Octavius with a curved dagger in an ornately worked eastern-silver sheath.

Probus translates.

'A poor gift, Antarah says.'

'But mine is poorer.'

Octavius hands him a small sandalwood box, inlaid with ivory and pearls.

Antarah mimes that he is not worthy of such a gift.

Tea is poured and at last conversation can begin. Even here, certain rituals have to be observed. Dialogue must at first be general, regarding weather, cattle and other such matters. At Hatim's camp Octavius learned one lesson early on. He wrote of it to Livia: that compliments are not welcome, they attract the evil eye. For this reason, many Arabs dress their children in poor clothes even though they have better. Allah is jealous.

The sun has set in the Valley of Tombs. A light breeze rattles the palms.

'Tell Antarah that his father was as my brother. I hope that he and I will be as kinsmen.'

'He says that you are his father.'

Probus, as interpreter, is now sitting a little behind, between the two.

'He is saying now that the women are not welcome to his people.'

'Why?'

Probus hesitates.

'They are bad women who will bring temptation and anger. He asks that you send them away.'

Octavius sighs.

'Explain to him, Probus, that if we send them away they will die. They have suffered and are deserving of mercy.'

Antarah shrugs.

'He says death is nothing but a going to Allah. Who will judge and punish.'

'Tell him that I ask him to trust me, as a son.'

There is a dangerous moment. Octavius allows himself no expression but he holds his breath. He senses that Otto at his shoulder has his hand on his knife. The Bedouin's temper is even shorter than the ordinary Arab's. Antarah's dark eyes are unreadable. He cannot imagine his face cracking in laughter like Hatim's. It is wearying to be starting all over again.

'Well, what is he saying?'

'He says that you, his father, are an honourable man.'

'Tell him that I have another son, of my blood. I would give up my life for him. And for the son of Hatim.'

For the moment it appears that the problem is shelved. Octavius's servant brings round sweetmeats. Imru snatches at them. More tea is poured. Octavius says he hears that Antarah is soon to be married. He wishes him many sons.

At last the boy smiles and his eyes brighten.

Octavius thinks how young he is.

It is past midnight when Antarah takes his leave. Imru has to be nudged awake.

Octavius, watching them ride away, feels the heaviness of his years. He misses Hatim more than he has ever done since the old chief's death.

He dismisses Otto and Probus, and his servant, but he can't sleep. That rattle of the palms when nothing else moves so often heralds a wind from the desert.

He takes the seal from his drawer.

Honour, he thinks, remembering the schoolroom and Gaius Germanicus. *Honestas* the moral virtue, not to be confused with *honos*.

Whoever in the real world can live by honour?

The General weighs the seal in his hand. Lead. He holds it up to the candlelight. The inscription reads: Imperator Octavius Augustus. Ridiculous. Did they cast several, he wonders, or just the one, hoping to lure me back?

And why me? Perhaps they imagine they perceive *honestas* in my dullness. The best candidate for the purple may be the one who least wants to wear it.

And then there is duty. Another heavy word. If the odds were not so long I might have felt it to be my duty.

Octavius's old wound stabs when he tips his face to look at the stars. He knows many of their names now and their places. Severus taught him soon after he arrived. That was the morning of our time in Tadmor.

He envies the ancients who could read their destinies in the night sky, trace the paths of the gods.

Octavius sees the sagging moon, half run in its waning, and flicks the seal, like a coin, into the air but there is no throwing it away, it falls at his feet. At least there are no odds on heads or tails. A shooting star arcs through the sky. It comes from Perseus in the north-east. To the old Romans this would have been a portent. Octavius knows better but he is still, like a child, amazed.

8

Octavius, my love, can you forgive me?

I'm writing this by candlelight just as though you could read it, because I need to.

It was Gaius Germanicus who betrayed us and it was my fault. I went to him after the priest who baptised Paulina was arrested. The Terror was at its height. Lucius Tarquinius had declared you a traitor. I hear he now calls himself Emperor.

Gaius Germanicus is odious. I know you were fond of him, in a way, but I have always detested him and probably not hidden my feelings very well. You know how impatient I am.

But he was your tutor, close to your family for so long. He put his fat hand on mine and said he had always had great hopes for you. He regretted the current circumstances but insisted that at such great times the individual must submit his will to that of the state.

Of course, I lost my temper and said I couldn't agree. All I asked was to follow you into exile. Failing that, protection for Paulina and myself.

He talked for half an hour then told me to go home to my child. He would make any arrangements that seemed necessary.

A Christian friend came that night. He warned me that my arrest was imminent. He was fleeing himself and brought me here – a long and dangerous journey.

So we are safe, I think. We have companionship and protection here. It's beautiful. These are good people. But I have to admit, as one year becomes two and now five, I find less comfort than I did in these friends. I am a bad Christian. My will is too strong. I find it increasingly hard to endure this exile from life. Father Jerome would say that life is everywhere Christ is and Christ is everywhere.

It is just as well I have little time to think. I pray with them and pray to have my faith confirmed within me.

Paulina is a busy happy child who looks at me sometimes through your grave eyes.

I must not think of Rufus. When he was a child and hurt himself, it was so easy to hold him and wipe away his pain. I can't stop myself imagining that he could be in agony now and I'm helpless to help him. Then, and only then, I hide myself and cry. You know how rarely I weep.

This is a letter full of self-pity. I'm ashamed of it.

So I'll tell you something good and cheerful though perhaps a little crazy. I've begun to think that I can hear your voice. Not clearly and only in snatches – at my shoulder when I'm milking and once in the olive grove.

Another time I woke in the night and saw you standing just inside the door. You bent over Paulina and smiled and then you were gone.

Marriage is a fine word, isn't it, for our love? Steady and rich and ripe. Sometimes I think, it is stronger than both of us and like our children could outlive us both.

9

Well, that's it then. There'll be no going home for anyone. And if you ask Otto, that's because there's no home to go to.

The General's given us as much of the truth as he sees fit and he's right. Whatever the whole of it is, he knows the men couldn't take it. Even as it is, we could have mutiny or desertion on our hands. Lieutenant Probus asked me and I told him, there could be trouble with the whores but they're the lesser of evils. It's only them, the heat and the sickness that's keeping the stopper on – and the respect they've still got for the General.

But they're low. It's only natural. No relief, no back-pay even if they had anything to spend it on. The bloody sun and the shits. And I can't be the only one who knows we haven't been told everything. No one half in his right mind is going to credit that Tivoli would send a senator alone into the desert to tell us we've got to stick it out, sorry. Poor sod, he's dead, whoever he was.

So I've got the men who can stand up as busy as I can. A good clean-out of the garrison block. One squad detailed to paint the mud-brick houses in the new city. Sulphur baths to clear up their sores.

Supplies are going to be a problem soon. We're relying already too much on the Bedouin. There's been trouble there. One of their women met a whore on the road to the new city and spat at her. There was a proper cat-fight. As if we hadn't got enough with the tarts scrapping among themselves. Now they've got their strength back there's no stopping them. Nayra says it's the heat. I've told her to make sure they wash.

All we need now is whores' diseases.

As for the Bedouin, I'm not too keen myself on that youngster who's taken over from Hatim. Never thought I'd miss that smelly old bugger but I've got to admit his word was law. He and the General had a real understanding, though don't ask me in what language. So it worked out, they didn't bother us and we didn't bother them.

That boy's too young and, if you ask me, he's got no real authority. Can't even control his own sister. Manah. She goes where she likes. She's got the shape of a woman now and she's naturally graceful, like their women are. She's only a child. She doesn't know what she's doing. But the way she walks, the sway of those hips, you'd say she's asking for it and it's only thanks to the whores she's not been raped. And you can imagine the consequences of that. Wouldn't mind putting my hand up that red skirt. I've even see the General looking at her though I've got to say, he was always nice to her when she was a kiddie and he was missing his own.

And don't we all, those of us who are family men. I'll admit that's half the reason I go to Nayra when I can. Those children – they could have broken your heart when they first came. Now they're brighter and they've got Otto sized up quick. I only have to show my face and they're after me. Grubby faces but eyes the colour of toffee and so full of life you'd never believe what they've been through. I always find something to take them.

Funny about children. They can drive you mad but they give you hope. I suppose that's what it is.

This bloody heat. It's only nine in the morning and already there's no air to breathe.

If it doesn't break something will happen, mark my word. There were shooting stars last night, a whole shower of them.

The women say the blue the Savages paint themselves with is some sort of magic against the heat. I'll believe that when I see it. All the same, it makes you think.

* * *

In the barracks the men have tied Flaminius to his bunk. He has stopped shouting. His painted eyelids flutter. They no longer torment him. A boy with a limp, to whom Flaminius used to give his services free, gets him to take some water with honey and washes his face, empties the bottle of urine. Flaminius has lost so much flesh his barrelled ribs appear like those of a ship.

'Severus? You remember when you arrived? We were going to dig up the whole of Tadmor, weren't we? I wonder what we hoped to find.'

These are the first voices Octavius heard when he walked in the Valley of Tombs: Kithoth, Iamlichu, Banai, Laascha, Arraum, Hairan, Sabeis, Elascha, Julius Aurelius Bolma, Elahbel, Shaqai, Moqimo, Maani, Athenathau, Atenatan, Hairan, Bolha, Breiki.

All the dead in the underground hypogea and the tower tombs. Severus had brought books and they found the names there. A few portrait busts outstared eternity, as alive and yet as mysterious and alien as the faces they had dug up in the museum. But most were names and no more than that.

Only later, when Tivoli fell silent, did Octavius walk alone in the necropolis and hear these names whispered aloud, so that the whole valley was peopled. I am Iamlichu, I am Bohla, we have stayed in the silence and darkness in patience. We are the wistful dead.

After their excavation of the museum, in the morning of their time at Tadmor, on a bright spring day, Octavius and Severus paused, poised. They were torn between the city of life and the valley of death.

As Octavius flicks his seal, the night of the shooting stars, he remembers that Severus stood in Diocletian's camp and tossed a coin. Heads for the city, tails for the Valley.

'Tails it is.'

Octavius and Severus are standing in the same spot. Before the day's heat they have been to the stables. A foal was born last night, to be named Star after the shooting stars. From the other side of the yard Dido sees Octavius and is jealous. She calls out and kicks at her stall.

'What do you make of Antarah, sir? Probus doesn't seem too sure.'

'He's young, obviously, but not stupid. As yet, I'd say there's no trust. We'll have to feel our way. The only danger in his youth is that he'll feel the need to prove himself.'

But the General's mind is not on the Bedouin. He is remembering.

'Those were great days, weren't they.'

Severus nods. Sometimes he feels as old as the General. As though his life before coming to Tadmor had been a brief dream. He had been born and then opened his eyes here in this improbable oasis, this forest of golden columns.

As far as Severus is concerned, his true life started in Tadmor and may well finish here; perhaps at the hands of the Blue Warriors, or from hunger or mutiny or sickness.

He doesn't think very much about that end. Not that Severus is any more the youth who expected, as youth does, to break the rules and live for ever. It is simply that his soul, or his sensibilities, or ordinary human consciousness, have become entwined like a vine with this place. And, he realises at this moment, with the destiny of the General.

Octavius shades his eyes with his hand.

Time shifts in this greedy, hard light that digests all colours.

He sees the two of them, having tossed the coin, walking into the Valley of Tombs. It was spring. The air and the light were young. Otto and a private followed them, carrying shovels and other tools. They were amateurs. They had Severus's books but no one here was an archaeologist. They had to tread carefully.

They left behind spring flowers and bird-song and date

palms that will live 200 years. A buzzard hung in the empty air above the Valley. Since the last diggings here the sand had swept in and piled up against the doors of the tower tombs, filled the mouths of the underground sepulchres, the hypogea.

Severus had books and maps. He had charted the south-west necropolis.

The silence was at first a little alarming. They were such a short distance from the bustle of the encampment, yet it might not have existed.

They were excited but anxious, to find but not to break.

After all, it was not so difficult. Time had heaped up sand, not stone. The tomb of the Three Brothers opened to them.

It was here that Octavius first hears the names of Malé, Saadai and Naamain.

Otto held the torch. He regarded the whole exercise as absurd, messing about in empty tombs. He had even heard that the air in these old graves can poison you. But he learned long ago to be dog-like in his patience. Of the two new lieutenants he favoured Probus. Severus struck him as girlish, too pretty by half.

'Look. These frescoes. Amazing.'

Severus took the torch from Otto. Octavius stepped forward to join him. He saw flowers and the face of Ganymede, stolen by Zeus to be his cup-bearer.

Deeper into the darkness and the silence, Octavius stood for the first time before the figure of Achilles, dressed in women's clothing, hiding from his destiny among the daughters of Lycomedes.

Young Severus said Achilles was the symbol of the soul, who, in shedding the disguise of earthly clothes, went to eternal life.

'This is like nothing I've ever seen. All those conquerors. But they're so much themselves.'

Octavius watched Severus and smiled at his wonder. He too, was surprised. But for himself he felt breathless. These sepulchres were empty yet Octavius was aware of an immanence of crowding spirits: a breath on his cheek, a hand jostling his elbow, snatching his sleeve.

And such longing. What for?

Years later, he wonders if that spring morning he had caught a glimpse of his future self walking here through his own autumn, in the company of voices.

Further down the valley they found a hypogeum unmarked on Severus's map. It took the four of them to shift the stone.

Below, it appeared to be the usual T-shape but smaller and without inscriptions or portrait busts or frescoes.

'Nothing here,' Severus said.

'There?' Octavius pointed not to the vacant shelves but to a darkness where he saw for the briefest second the body of a girl hooped around a bundle of rags. And then Otto came forward with the torch and there was nothing, not so much as a footprint.

'You all right, sir?'

'The air. That's all.'

Octavius thought: we have revealed something that should not be seen before its time.

Octavius was gasping as they scrambled up into the day. He had dust in his eyes. He remembered Pausonias talking about cosmologists and their discovery that for a brief second the present might coincide with time to come. The tutor drew on the board something vaguely the shape of an hour-glass, one cone upon another. What did he call it? Octavius stumbled and remembered. Future light.

But then he was in the vegetable light of the spring city and in another country Gaius Germanicus banged the table and the General remembered: 'there is only the present, that is all we have.' And: 'there are no questions that cannot be answered'.

Severus was jubilant.

'There's so much. There is no end to it here. This is how Aurelian last saw it. It's hardly changed. Don't you think, sir?'

'I wonder sometimes if we shouldn't leave the dead in peace.'

'But they're not there. There's no one.'

That evening Octavius wrote to Livia.

Our amateur excavations in the Valley of Tombs began today. In all we found three hypogea and entered two tower tombs. With some it was an easy matter of clearing away the sand. Others were blocked with stone and rubble but Otto and another soldier worked hard with pick-axe and shovel. In fact, we all worked together. I daresay a real excavator would have been horrified at the use of the pick-axe. I think Otto disapproved of the whole enterprise but he will put his shoulder to anything. And Severus is excellent company: so keen. He has lent me the books he brought and he noted every find and detail. We have agreed that once we have done all we can we should seal the tombs again as we have no idea of the effect of air and sand on the frescoes.

You remember, my darling, how we trudged through the necropolis of Thebes? The tombs here are not as remarkable, the carving is good but the frescoes are comparatively crude, after the Egyptian. In a way, I like that. They seem fresher and less pompous. There is one carving you would enjoy. It shows the sacred meal which seems so much a part of the cult of the dead – and two small children presenting their father with flowers as he lies on a couch. You can see the Hellenistic influence but it does not take over.

And there is another difference. So many feet have tramped through the Egyptian sepulchres there is little feeling of awe. Here, I at least, had a sense of violation.

There was something else. Perhaps it is the lonely desolation of the Valley but although I was exhilarated by our discoveries, I was aware of something desperate or pitiful about these elaborate graves. They suggest to me a terror of death which, in turn, implies an uncertainty of resurrection. It is the same with the Egyptians but in their valley of death you step from the tomb immediately into a place of living villages, touts, children, cultivated fields, cheerful grave-robbers.

I must admit that although I argued with Gaius Germanicus about Lucretius I have never given much thought to the idea of life everlasting after death. (I know you have but this is not the place to speak of it.) The stoic culture of the new Romans has suited me well enough. I like the world and work to do and rest at the end of the day; which is probably how I see death.

Perhaps I envy the Moslems a little. For them life is a short dream, the end of it no more than a release into a better world. This makes them fearless in battle, philosophical in life, like the Bedouin chief Hatim I am getting to know and respect.

But if our culture is right and Gaius Germanicus knows the truth, why was I so affected by our diggings this morning? I think perhaps it was a fantasy to be put down to claustrophobia, that the souls of Malé, Saadai and Naamain and all the others, and their wives and mothers and children, are stranded within those hills, in a terrible country between death and final extinction or eternity. And very nearly, I can hear them speak.

Thinking about these people and their terror of extinction helps me to understand better the purpose of those ancient eastern religions I find so barbaric. The Zoroastrians, for instance, and the Mithraic blood baptism, when the initiate lay in a trench under the slaughtered bull. And for that matter the Christian myth, which is bloody enough.

But blood then was the symbol of life. I look at the remains of the sacrificial altar in the Sanctuary of Bel, where I have set up summer camp, and I begin to grasp that in all these cults the design was to return God's gift of life to him and so ensure immortal life.

So in the ancient Persian cult the soul was freed from the body to rise to the seventh sphere. And I study my Bedouin prayer-mat with its formalised star pattern and then gaze up at the night sky and imagine I can see what they saw: the seven spheres of Moon, Mercury, Venus, the Sun, Mars, Jupiter and Saturn, all circles through which the soul descended at birth and, given the necessary rites, flew up at death to everlasting life. Like Achilles in the hypogeum, putting off his shabby disguise.

To understand is not to say that I believe. I am still repelled by the altar in the Sanctuary and the thought of what must have taken place there. Sometimes at night I feel the breath of the pagan past unpleasantly close. It has a dark smell. As a soldier I have tried and failed to staunch too many wounds to accept that the spilling of blood can be anything but ugly, death anything but the end of life.

I look forward to the morning in Tadmor. Unlike some ruins, the city of limestone is not mournful. There is an amazing sense of life here. And as at Azraq and Aswan I am more aware of the old Romans and their enterprise than I ever was in Rome.

Livia, I have re-read this letter and I shan't send it. You will think I'm depressed when I know quite well I shall be cheerful again tomorrow.

I don't believe the Savages are any immediate threat. So you will come and we'll see all this together.

So I'll put these pages in with the private journal I have started to keep – as distinct from the daily army log. Then, if you are in the world without me and see this, I shall be talking to you from beyond the grave and that will be the only immortality I could wish.

In present time in the furious heat of midsummer Octavius watches the new foal stagger to her feet on surprised legs and snuffs up the smell of horse, so comfortable to him.

He puts his hand on the lieutenant's shoulder.

'Walk with me, Severus.'

In the street of the Great Colonnades the garrison goes about its daily business. Although fraternisation with Bedouin women is forbidden, their small children, trailing infants and dogs, play and beg among the soldiery. And the old women, squatting in what shade they can find, sell sweetmeats or simply raise their hands in shrill imprecations, for alms in the name of Allah. The men used to bargain for cloths and carved camels and shiny bracelets to take home. Now, if they give, it is out of pity.

The men step back and salute but the children are not impressed by the General. They shriek and dance and play grandmother's footsteps in his wake.

'Hatim told me that his people are going back to the old gods. I wonder how Antarah will deal with that.'

The General has also permitted a weekly market. From the agora to their right as they walk between the Colonnades, they can hear the shouts. Otto always keeps an eye open in case of trouble but so far there has been nothing serious. Chickens and meat are sold, sometimes a goat; not that the army has much to barter with nowadays. They have medal ribbons, the day's issue of rations, a few trinkets. It is a court-martial offence to pilfer from stores. Some of the older men have books. The Bedouin prefer them illustrated. They always want to know if they are holy.

Once, in the early days, there was an alert when strangers rode in from the south. In the desert light a man mounted on a camel appears as one tall beast, a company of them a supernatural army forming eerily in the air. This is how the Blue Warriors are expected to arrive.

But it was only Jafnah, a cousin of Hatim's with camels for sale: an occasion for celebration and bargaining.

They made an exotic spectacle, these wild-looking nomads from the desert with their rifles and richly worked and coloured camel-packs. The men regarded them with curiosity and some suspicion. Octavius sent Probus to haggle for camels and returned with him that evening at Hatim's invitation.

He remembers now the talk around the fire that evening,

of the excellence of Jafnah's camels who could outrun any other camels in the whole of Arabia.

Jafnah had a villainous appearance but treated Octavius with the same courtesy as did Hatim. He had a glaucoma of one eye but the other was sharp enough. Octavius had the feeling he was being tested, perhaps mocked a little but without malice.

Probus interpreted.

'He is asking if the General can ride a camel.'

'I learned when I was young, in Egypt.'

Hatim smiled. Jafnah threw up his hands.

'The Egyptian camel is a poor creature, as is his master. Our camels are of a light colour from the desert around Wadi Rum. Our females will ride for ever until they die beneath you. The true Bedouin are great breeders of camels. Does the General know the name of camel in our tongue?'

'It is jamal, which is from the word for beautiful. Tell him that I have been in Wadi Rum. It is a good place. I have it in my heart.'

'The General is wise, a good scholar.'

'Thank our friend and ask him if he has seen others in the desert.'

This appeared to be a less welcome question. There was a silence and some shrugging and for a moment Octavius thought that Jafnah would not give him an answer. He had come across this phenomenon before among Arabs: a vagueness like a veil drawn across the face when they do not like the question. But finally the visitor decided to answer.

'There are no Bedouin but us between here and Rum. The jinn are not seen. They come out of the air and our tribes are gone on the wind. They are dust. I do not know about the south. Even the water of Azraq is poisoned. There is no life for our people.'

'I am sorry. May Allah protect them.'

Later, the mood changed again. Jafnah was joking at his cousin's expense.

'So our noble relation is no longer Bedouin. He has become one of the settled who grow crops and sheep and horses like peasants, fellahin.'

Hatim shrugged. He would not be offended. By the morning, even before the garrison stirred, the visitor was gone. Only Octavius, waking early and strolling beyond the palm-grove, saw them go. He heard the voice of the nomads urging on their camels: hut-hut-hut. And then they were lost to sight in the desert, as if they had ridden into eternity and disappeared.

A child snatches at the corner of Octavius's cloak. An osmotic relationship appears to have developed between the garrison and the Bedouin. It is hard to imagine the survival of the one without the other.

This midsummer morning, the General picks up the small girl and holds her, laughing. She is startled out of her daring, struck dumb, eyes enormous. When he puts her down, gently, she runs. Octavius remembers Manah at the same age. He cannot imagine Paulina because he has never seen her, except in pictures before the mail stopped coming. And Livia sent a lock of her hair. It was coppery brown, like Livia's, but curly.

Octavius and Severus stroll after the child in the direction of the agora. There is more hawking of goods than buying. The young Bedouin women are not allowed to enter the encampment, so men and old women are displaying their wares: rugs and cushions, fleece, jewellery, pots.

Octavius smiles. If there are ghosts here, they are cheerful ones. He likes the smell of spices and goats and heat.

'You know we're asked to Antarah's wedding feast, Severus? We must go, of course. Not to do so would give offence.'

'Sir.'

It is midday. They walk down to the shade and cool of the stream.

The General stands. Severus waits. Tonight, where the sulphur stream emerges above ground, the air will be steamy, like mist.

Octavius is thinking how sturdy, organic, societies appear. And yet they are so precariously balanced, so fragile. One torn thread and the whole web is broken. Tivoli could be returned to dust by now. Tadmor tomorrow.

He feels the small dull weight of the seal in his pocket.

'Do you remember, in the Roman studies they pumped into our heads, *Invicta Roma Aeterna*? The empire was already falling apart yet they still hung onto their slogans. As if ideas can survive in thin air. Fleas need dogs, my tutor used to say. Pausonias the Macedonian. I wish you'd known him, Severus.'

'So do I, sir.'

Severus wishes. He does not know what he wishes. To take this weight from the General. Something heavy he is carrying.

In the distance, infinitely small in this light, against the columns of the city, a figure is herding a flock of black goats. The light dissolves the city. Voices carry clearly. The substance of flesh and of buildings is less certain.

Octavius says at last: 'You think I should have accepted their offer, don't you, Severus? March in rags and triumph to Tivoli?'

When he was younger, when he first arrived, Severus would have been startled. Now he thinks.

'I believe you would be trusted, sir.'

'It's a military impossibility, Severus. But thank you.' The General looks directly at the lieutenant. 'You see, Severus, I'm a dog without fleas.'

For one second Severus imagines the unthinkable: that he might reach out and in his own flesh take some of the burden of loneliness from the General.

Then a palm rattles, a stone is dislodged and gathers

pebbles on its way down to the stream.

Octavius feels the earth tilt beneath his feet. As he falls the white exhausted sky seems to fall with him.

10

Tied to his bunk, Flaminius rides the tremor. He sees a plate and a tin mug slide across the barrack-room table, as they might when a boat heels on the ocean. He cries out but no one hears. In his fever he believes that he will die if he lies here and plucks at the lengths of cloth that bind him.

It was a small quake. The shock to the system of the garrison is out of proportion, an indication of the fragility of morale.

The city fell once before to an earthquake but few know of this. Severus knows. Octavius knows. Neither speaks of it but it is in their minds all day. They are alert.

Octavius is bruised more than cut. Severus put out his arm and broke the General's fall. The tremor was followed by a wind. They walked back to the city holding their cloaks in front of their eyes against the sand. Just as abruptly, the wind ceased and it was hard to breathe.

Even in the brief dusk the dogs still bark and the horses are restless. A full minute before the tremor they had screamed, tried to break out of their stalls. One damaged a tendon. The camels lost their grand indifference.

From his tent Octavius hears the dogs. He sits at his table, the General in his solitude, reading Lucretius on the subject of earthquakes: the fear men have that the earth may be snatched from under their feet, the world robbed of its foundation. This is what happened, Lucretius says, in Syrian Sidon and at Aegium in the Peloponnese.

Lucretius understood the peculiar terror of such catastrophes.

Let them go on imagining that sky and earth are indestructible and destined to life everlasting, he said.

But the voice was that of Gaius Germanicus.

Rain ran down the school-room windows. There had been snow that winter in Tivoli.

'So you see, although he was himself an Epicurean, Lucretius is generous. He allows for human weakness and self-deception.'

Young Fidus Octavius was thinking: but what if the world is indestructible? What if there is everlasting life? But the bench was hard, the room was cold, he wanted to go home. And he had learned the pointlessness of arguing with Gaius Germanicus.

Now, reluctantly, he would tend to agree with him.

Everything points to extinction.

He rubs his stubbled chin. Grey whiskers nowadays. The candle flickers but is steady again. Just a breeze.

The strange thing was that falling this morning, as the sky tipped and the earth came up, he had felt no fear, nothing but thankfulness that everything was done. It was like the dive and the dream, the bottomless pool at Tivoli, but without the suffocating terror. Like a man catching his breath after a race, he would have swum on down for ever in company with the muddy sacred fish, his guide.

Then Severus caught his elbow and Octavius was stranded on the earth again, gravid, stunned.

Young Fidus Octavius knew that his mother worried about the lack of paternal influence.

When he thought of the father he had never seen he used to imagine Arabia. Arabia Perdita, it was called by then, east of Egypt and from Aqaba south.

Idly, the young schoolboy drew on the map, where Arabia was lost: a camel, a horse, a tank, a palm-tree. He coloured the desert yellow, the palm-tree green, the horse and the tank brown. Then he added a stick-man standing up in the tank and a big yellow sun.

He imagined his father riding in his tank up the side of a sand-dune and down the other. His mother had told him that the desert was cold at night, colder than Tivoli. Fidus Octavius frowned. He could not imagine a cold desert.

Gaius Germanicus's ruler whacked him across the knuckles, not for the first time.

Fidus Octavius bit his lip. He would not show his pain. He would not cry. He was seven.

His mother Helena worried that the boy was so contained. He was strong, he had friends, he played with other boys, but he did not seem to need them. Sometimes he looked at her with her dead husband's eyes: gentle and yet somehow measuring. Gaius Germanicus said the boy was doing well enough. It was important not to spoil him.

Fidus Octavius continued to invent his father. There were pictures of him in Tivoli but Fidus Octavius did not believe that man was his father. His father was in the desert. The desert was made of sand, like the beach at Ostia, but it went on as far as you could see. You had to have a map and a compass and to know how to take bearings by the sun. His father knew all about that, and scorpions and snakes and how to find water.

Helena bought him a book about deserts, with illustrations. He could read most of it and was particularly interested in mirages, once they were explained to him. It seemed to him at first impossible that you could see something that wasn't there – an oasis, an enemy army, a city: all just pictures the light made.

When he was seven Fidus Octavius decided that everyone had made a mistake. His father was not dead but alive in Arabia Perdita, in one of those mirages. Gaius Germanicus said anything you saw with your eyes must be true. Fidus Octavius had the sense not to mention mirages.

* * *

The General is drily touched by his younger self. It is dark. He has had Dido tethered outside his tent. She was afraid of the earth tremor. She is not so young now.

Octavius yawns and blinks. There is another child: Rufus, new-born at Aswan, smelling of milk, waving his small hands like sea-flowers. And then he is gone, it is too late to call him back and Livia is angry and bereaved.

At the age of twelve Fidus Octavius admitted to himself that his father was dead and he could not forgive him for dying. For being death, down there where the old fish waits and the spring feeds the dark pool.

For a while he even blamed his mother. She should have stopped his father from dying. He was never rebellious but he drew further apart from her.

He blamed himself, too. If he were better his father would not have left him.

Now Octavius looks back at the boy who was himself; he sees him standing in the doorway, the sun behind him, impatient to swim, while his mother Helena sits with her sewing on her lap, against a blue-white wall. That is all he sees: the picture without words, the woman in a long skirt sitting in a high-backed chair; the correctness of the marble-flagged floor, grey and white, grey and white. There is a small yellow bird in a cage.

When he was younger he would have kissed her before he left. But he is twelve now.

Perhaps it is because he lacked a father that the voices of Gaius Germanicus and Pausonias are so insistent.

Helena was happier in her old age. Livia loved her. She saw more of Rufus than he did himself.

And then Fidus Octavius was a man. He saw the desert and imagined it closing in silence around his father.

Gaius Germanicus pointed to the coloured map on the wall. He must have been young then but already his hands were over-fleshed, his rings bit into his fingers.

'All those deserts were once under the sea.'

In battle there was little time for imaginings. But Octavius has often seen in a mirage, an incoming tide.

These last years at Tadmor he has looked in his mind at deserts he has known: Sahara's great waves of soft dunes, Arabia's cliffs, lion-coloured Sinai and the black sea-bed of Syria's sands. And the season when springs gush from the earth to pour down the wadis, drawing out flowers. In this miracle he perceives a memory of greater waters, a prelapsarian age when fish swam in these sands and the lost animals roamed fertile plains. Lion, gazelle, leopard. And do the sea-creatures looking down from their flat eyes, through water-light, spy us creeping awkwardly across the ocean floor?

Dido is fussing. The General closes Lucretius, blows out his candle and eases himself heavily from his chair. He goes out to comfort the mare and lays his cheek against her, smelling horse and dust. She muzzles him, velvety, then throws back her head in alarm.

'Who's that?'

'Otto, sir. Just been doing another check. No one hurt, no structural damage. A few stones in the ruins, that's all.'

'Good.'

'Flaminius has gone missing. I don't know if you could say deserted. He was half off his head. Can't believe he got far.'

'Send a couple of men in daylight. The Homs road and the desert. But they're to take no risks.'

'Lieutenant Probus has already given the orders, sir.'

Octavius nods.

'The women?'

'We had a bit of trouble with them but they're settled now. Queer things, earthquakes. Shake everyone up. It's like an enemy you can't see, I suppose. And you're waiting to see if there'll be another. I'll take Dido back to the stables, shall I, sir?'

'Thank you, Otto.'

Otto seems disinclined to leave.

'Was there something else, sergeant?'

'What you said to the men, sir, about our posting being extended. I've been wondering. Can I ask, sir, is that orders from Tivoli?'

There is no shower of stars tonight. Cloud has come in. The sky is black.

'I'm not sure you can ask, Otto. But for your information only, we're on our own.'

'I see, sir.'

Octavius smiles.

'We're a long way, aren't we, Otto, from the night you were on guard duty at the villa?'

'We are, sir.'

In the night there is another tremor, but very slight. Some sleep through it under the heavy sky.

The General wakes, sweating, from a dream of falling, or diving. He dreams he is suffocating. There is no safe place. The earth is a cliff.

Something? A scrabble of stones? An animal outside?

Octavius lights his candle, scrabbling for matches. A book has fallen from a shelf. He touches the gun he keeps on his side-table.

Those shadows just within the tent-flap are alive.

Sweat runs down into his eyes. This is fever weather. There is the scent of musk, a finger on his lips, crinkly hair.

She blows out the candle but he has seen her face.

'Manah. What is it? What are you doing here?'

He tries to stand and remembers he is naked. He is dizzy as he was when he fell by the stream. The girl cannot support his weight. Octavius sinks back onto the mat and cushions that make up his bed.

'Was it another quake? Manah, you should not be here. You must go.'

He wipes the sweat from his eyes with his forearm.

Livia? Paulina?

It is like being at sea. Any moment the deck may pitch and throw you down.

He tries to force himself up on his elbows. It is a terrible battle one has with gravity.

Lips graze his open palm.

Desire and despair, fear and longing, such longing and loneliness, are shapes cut from shadows that rush now together.

In the new city many of the men have risked a charge by staying overnight with the women, who are afraid, and cling to them, begging not to be left.

Probus is awake at once: he has a capacity for instant awareness that is the legacy of anyone who has been on campaign.

In his quarters, Severus feels the boy who comes to him from time to time, turn in his arms and wake frightened.

'It's nothing. It's over already.'

Severus kisses the sweetest spot at the base of the throat where a pulse beats.

'You can't understand me, can you?'

He disentangles himself and gives the boy a slap on the bottom.

'Off you go. You're going to ruin my reputation one day.'

The boy pulls on his thobe – the long, dress-shaped tunic – and folds a kiffayah around his head and half across his face. He waits. His bare feet are grubby.

Severus yawns.

'Ah, yes. The present.'

Quite soon he will have nothing left to give. He wonders what will happen then.

Meanwhile, he finds a handkerchief, pure linen and embroidered with his own initial.

When he opens his eyes again the boy is still there.

'So what is it now?'

The boy mimes, speaks.

'Ali. Oh, Ali. If you're talking about love, I don't know. Come here. Let me kiss you. There. Now run on home. No more presents tonight. Enough.'

Although he is weary Severus cannot sleep. He reaches under his mattress for the diary he has kept spasmodically since he arrived. He pours a glass of wine and flicks through the pages.

With only four officers left, he and Probus have comfortable quarters in Diocletian's camp. The structure is of golden limestone collected from the outskirts of the ruined city. The floor too is stone. Severus has added bright Bedouin rugs, brass candlesticks, a copper tray and brass coffee-pot with a straight handle and domed lid. In this his servant makes him coffee such as the Bedouin drink, unsweetened, with cardamom. He has hung some rugs on the walls. In winter there is a fleece for his bed. When he wishes it he has company at night. Such a relief after Tivoli, where the Greek way, so-called, was deplored, though practised, Severus knew, in high places.

The air is heavy. A small lizard looks frozen on the wall.

Severus leans against cushions at the bed-head and smiles at the early entries. His excitement at getting this posting, the even greater thrill of the first diggings with Octavius, excavating the museum, working in the Valley of Tombs.

As the years pass there are more references to the General. The first indicate respect and growing affection. Severus is impressed by Octavius's easy command, his way with the men.

Then Severus had written: he seems to me a lonely man. To some degree his rank makes this inevitable. But I wonder if, in any case, he might choose solitude? Though he appears to like my company. Can't think why. Perhaps because I'm an optimist? Lent him Catullus and we talked about Horace.

I doubt somehow if he has close friends of either sex. Except perhaps his wife.

He said he was struck by the friendship between Horace

and Maecenas. I dug out my copy. It's in the second book of Odes. *Cur me querelis*. I have taken no false oath: we shall go, we shall go, whenever you lead the way, comrades prepared to take the last journey together.

My father said he was a first-class soldier but not popular in the military command. A bit stiff, he said. Something like that.

. . . Can't imagine why but I think he quite enjoys it when I talk my nonsense. About the hypocrisy of our empire. The Concordia as a licence for conquest and greed. And the idiocy of the Roman studies at the Army Schools and the Academy. Horace censored. Catullus banned. Boring Julius Caesar. As if there'd been no history in between. The only thing that interests me about the Roman tacticians is what Caesar would have done if he'd had the fire-power that's tucked away in our silo.

. . . I asked the General about the campaigns in Africa and Arabia. Mombasa. Azraq. Keraq. He said, all you think, if you think at all, in any battle, is of home and peace and rest. He said you've got to think about death, being killed, what it means, before the fight. Work through the idea and then forget it. He got the wound in his neck in Africa. It bothers him sometimes. I bought some oil from the Bedouin that seems to help. Though I think it's more the massage. Or just being able to give way for a minute. For that short time he's a man. And then he's a general again.

. . . I know what the men think of me. I haven't been blooded. And they suspect the other thing. To which I'd say, I know what goes on in the barracks and what Flaminius is for.

. . . It's a peculiar word to use, but I think there is something innocent about the General. Or hurt?

There is the last entry, the new one.

He asked me what I thought. I said he'd make a good emperor, or something to that effect. So he would. But what I really meant was: if he doesn't get away from Tadmor he might go mad. That is, I imagine what it must be like, to be in command and obliged to sit out these years waiting for an enemy you never see. And now in exile as well, knowing you cannot go home.

I wish I could bring him his wife and children. Since I can't, I watch him setting off on his lonely walks into the Valley of Tombs, or scanning the desert for the Blue Warriors, and I long to reach out in the only human way of the flesh I know, from which I give and take comfort. But I can guess how that would repel him. It would also be an impertinence. What can I truly know of the longing behind those wide eyes? What visions he has?

So the lieutenant loves the general? Better not think about that. Hold Ali or his brother in your arms. *We shall go, we shall go, whenever you lead the way*. Perhaps. More likely not.

Then all I can do is to stand by and catch his elbow, break his fall.

I think of him hacked to death by Savages.

The diary slips to the floor. And the glass. Wine is spilled, staining the page the colour of blood. Severus sleeps. His abandoned body is beautiful. Sweat stains the pillow, sex the sheet.

The heat thickens. The sky is low and colourless. Six men are put on a charge and disciplined for absence without leave the night before in the new city with the whores. The whole camp is like a man with a fever. The stink from the latrines hangs in the air. Fights break out suddenly and violently. There have been no more tremors but there is a nervous after-shock. No man feels the ground to be solid beneath his feet. There are shouts of anger from the Bedouin camp. In the new city a whore has been beaten up but refuses to name her assailant. She is afraid of losing what security she has.

It is strange how the men are disturbed by the absence of Flaminius. They despised and abused him but he had become part of the functioning whole that made up the life of the barracks.

There is a rumour that the whores are sick, they are responsible for these ulcers and sores. But the men will still go to them. Sex is their only relief and comfort. They talk about little else. It is part of their fever.

At dawn Probus reports that the Bedouin have been terrified by the earthquake. Antarah is angry. His people are calling for the old gods to return. A prize ram has been found with its throat cut, not an ordinary slaughter: the man responsible has run mad, his face daubed with blood.

Octavius nods.

'Any sign of Flaminius?'

'No, sir.'

'Call Otto and get Dido saddled.'

Probus is startled to see Manah. She must have spent the night sleeping on the ground outside Octavius's tent.

'Send her away. Don't tell Antarah.'

There are times when the General has a face of stone.

He seems to look at the Bedouin girl without seeing her.

Soon after dawn two of the men leave the encampment by the road to Homs.

At the same time the General, with Otto beside him, rides out north-east into the desert in the direction of Dayr az Zawr. Otto carries a rifle. The General is unarmed.

Flies bother the air below the low sky. There is no sun. The light is sick.

The figures of the two horsemen shiver, shake, and the dubious light swallows them. They are gone.

11

Sometimes, walking in the Valley of Tombs at sunset, Octavius has heard the voices not of Iamlichu or Banai but of Pausonias the Macedonian and Gaius Germanicus, individually, or in dispute.

Pausonias's voice is that of the locust, dry, chafing, the crepitation of husky corn-wings.

'Eternity? Well, who knows? Anything is possible. We must accept all possibilities to question while admitting that we may never have the answers. Courage is in asking. The unquestioned life is not worth living.'

Pausonias is in the air all around and in the folding shadows.

Gaius Germanicus settles like a bluebottle.

'Ask me any question, you foolish boy. I can answer it. Our time on this earth is short, endurable, instructive. To dwell on death is morbid. It is a vegetable process. That is all.'

Gaius Germanicus buzzes in the voice of Plato's Adeimantus, arguing with Socrates.

'What use are philosophers to anyone? Hot air. Witterers. Fools and villains. And you imagine they should run the state?'

'No.' A sigh from Pausonias. 'You are putting the words of Plato into my mouth. The just state was an impossible fantasy. Government will always be in the hands of office-seekers. Men of your sort, Gaius Germanicus. But we are confusing the boy. He always had difficulty with Plato. Look at him. What do you see?'

A snort from Gaius Germanicus.

'A fool with too many questions in his head. He suffers

from a sentimental preoccupation with what he imagines to be his soul. History is inevitable. It will not wait for him to make up his mind.'

It is quiet now but a wind from the south has heaped up the sand. Octavius can wade no further but still he looks out, down the Valley, like a man standing on a beach, watching the ocean pile in.

Someone laughs.

'Pausonias?'

'Gaius never could stand laughter. Well, dog-soldier, you've come to the difficult questions, I think. Don't ask too much of yourself. He is right in one respect. The world can be beautiful. Look around.'

Octavius wants to ask why Pausonias let his life run out like that from the cut vein. Was he taking charge of his destiny or was he simply tired? How could he leave that wretched boy, his lover?

But the air is empty.

Turning back, Octavius sees the distant beacon of Otto's fire by the Arab castle. He makes his way, listening for the whisper of voices, between the long files of sentinel tombs.

How long ago was that? Years? Months? Looking back Octavius would have said that there were three figures in the Valley that night. Himself, following his father, his younger self, the boy, trying to measure his shorter legs to fit their prints.

I am not clever enough to formulate the questions, he thinks, and at the same time slackens the reins to let Dido pick her own way through the difficult terrain.

'Otto?'

'Sir?'

'The compass?'

'We're going north-east, sir. If Flaminius came this way he won't last long.'

It is true, this is an unpromising landscape for survival. What had once been a metalled road to Dayr az Zawr on the Euphrates has been all but reclaimed by the desert. Abandoned long ago by the Syrians, along with Tadmor, the surface has become rutted and cracked, eroded by frost, strewn with boulders and rocks. After rain stunted greenery and low-growing succulents force their way out to the light. So the road has deteriorated from a highway to a track that from time to time entirely disappears. Octavius and Otto ride not on it but alongside and still need their compass. The road has become an act of someone else's imagination, a line on a map which no longer bears any relation to reality.

And this desert is peculiarly spiteful: a barren, treeless plain,upon which, in this dangerous light, the abandoned armoury of old wars, rusting into the earth, appears suddenly: as a claw, a dead beast, an iron tree. You could stumble once and cut yourself to death here.

'We might have done better with camels, sir,' Otto says. This is a concession from him. He has always regarded the camel with suspicion, as something eccentrically put together, invested with dubious qualities of temper; all the while, though, respecting its usefulness. Does it not have nostrils that will close against a sandstorm? An amazing capacity for endurance and for travelling without water?

But respect is the end of Otto's tolerance. He has never taken part in the camel races with the Bedouin that the General seems to enjoy. And today has chosen to ride his usual horse: piebald and sturdy, heavy, with the look almost of a cart-horse to the withers, short but useful legs, an unresponsive mouth but enough common sense to make up for its lack of sensitivity.

They make an odd couple: the General on flighty Dido, her nerves somehow responsive to his will before he has even twitched the reins. And three hands lower at least, a dozen paces behind, Otto watchful on his fairground mount.

The General reins in Dido. They pause to eat sandy dates and take a drink from their water-flasks.

It is an effort to breathe in this air, full of sand although you cannot see it, a strain on the lungs. So they do not speak.

Octavius remembers early sorties in this direction before fuel became something precious, to be conserved.

His orders had been to hold Tadmor. On no account to challenge the Savages at the Euphrates. Already by then, the boundaries of the empire were being redrawn. Southern Arabia was gone along with most of Africa. With diminished airpower, supply lines to Tivoli were dangerously short. The Savages, engaged, would undoubtedly attempt to draw the empire forces across the Euphrates into the land now lost that had once been man's first garden, Mesopotamia; and beyond that, Persia, Iran. Like a wistful ghost the old name of Persia was still recorded faintly on the map; as a country of the mind which might in fantasy be regained, at the point in the cosmologists' twin cones where future light and past light meet.

But this was an idea of a place. A fancy unfit for soldiers, of a wonder that perhaps had never been.

Pausonias, conducting his history seminar at the Academy, had spoken with irony of old Rome in her decline, falling before the Visigoths but dreaming still of Babylon, Parthia, Persia, the Ganges.

Like a man in senile dementia, Pausonias said.

So as death approached, Rome lived in complacent fantasy.

Octavius blinks. He is in the Academy garden.

It was high summer. The boys sat on the grass. The sun dazzled. It was hard to make out Pausonias's narrow face in the shade. Fidus Octavius tried to imagine what it would be like, old age, the body worn out but the mind still weaving its dreams. Once, when he was very small, on holiday at Fiesole, his grandfather was dozing after lunch under the fig-tree. He snored. And he was talking to someone. And then in his sleep he slapped his cheek. The hornet stung him. The small boy was afraid of something that had been formless but took on the shape of a hornet. He remembers running to get as far away from the old man as he could. He fell and scratched his hand on a rose. He has the thorn in his flesh still.

Pausonias said once: if you see history coming then cover your head and hide.

Octavius opens his eyes. The two riders move on. Otto thinks, there has been a change in the General. What is it?

The piebald stumbles. Otto lets her find her feet. He swears. When he looks up again the General is a vague, disappearing shape, a mythic creature on Dido's four legs, foolish on the road to a fabled river, pressed between earth and sky. No more than a scrawl now, riding on.

Otto kicks his mount into a faster jog-trot.

What possessed the General to go after Flaminius himself? Countermanding Probus's orders. In Otto's opinion it would have been a waste of a common soldier, chasing after a dead man.

The Bedouin call this a bad way, possessed by jinns. Not that Otto credits such rubbish. But you've got to admit there's often something real behind that kind of talk. That is, people give their fears the names of bogies. It's human.

Nayra wasn't so well this morning. She had a sweat. I left her sleeping.

I'll tell you, all these years I've never known the General give an order I'd argue with. Until today.

There's something blank about his eyes.

It was on this road, on an early sortie, Captain Drusus disappeared with three of the men, on a clear day, not a cloud, you could see for miles. He was in an armoured car. That was all that was left, as if the Savages had made themselves invisible. There were no tracks, no sign of struggle. A few weeks later one of the missing men was dumped on the road outside the camp, his balls stuffed in his mouth.

'Sir?' He has come up level with the General.

'Do you reckon, sir, that the Savages are like the Tuareg? It's the indigo dye in their cloth that rubs off?'

'Quite possibly.'

'Some of the women say they are veiled. Others that they ride naked except for a loin-cloth. The only thing they agree on is that they are giants.'

'People make giants out of anything they most dread, don't you think, Otto?'

Otto nods.

Octavius feels that soon he will ride up against a block, an end. As though such air as there is will close against him. It is an act of will to continue.

This morning he had felt driven from the encampment and yet afraid to leave it. The fear has ridden with him. It takes his breath. And then he thinks: if I could see its face it would be my own.

I am afraid of myself.

Otto glances at the General. He looks sick.

They stop.

'Give me the map, Otto.'

They dismount and crouch by a thorn-bush. It is amazing, Octavius reflects how a terrain looks empty and yet how busy it is. A black pebble appears to move. It is a beetle. A lizard freezes but his amber eye gives him away. There are small, star-shaped white flowers waiting for the rains, insects Octavius cannot name in the dry grass, a file of ants from a mound disturbed by Dido's hoof; and then the thorns rattle and a bird no bigger than a wagtail but duller in colour flies from the bush. There is no such thing as stasis. Nothing is ever still. Life re-forming, scattered, regrouping, renewing, inventing itself in fresh shapes. There is something heartening about this. They have disturbed, damaged even, an immensely complex social order. Still, it will imagine and build itself again.

Octavius traces the map with his finger.

'You see. Araq, Suknah, there are springs all along this route. Oases. Wadis. We saw it when we first came. You remember, Otto? As green as home.'

Under the sweating sky the General's skin looks too dry, Otto judges.

'And somewhere in this direction – here – there is a lost palace. Off the road. It will be north, I think.'

Otto scratches his head.

'A palace, sir?'

'Perhaps a city once.'

The General's eyes have lost that dullness. They are too bright now. He sees something beyond the range of Otto's vision or imagining.

It is noon. The sun has lost its circumference. It bleeds into the sky. The horizon is lost. You might see anything you fancied: Savages, lakes, oceans, cities, palaces.

There had been so much to do in Tadmor Octavius had paid little attention when Hatim mentioned the site, years ago. But the idea settled in his mind; from a vague thought it has been working over the years, putting on towers and courts, gardens, fountains. Paradise.

'It could be Roman. Built on by the Ommayads. Perhaps not far off the route to the Euphrates. You see?'

Otto looks. He sees nothing on the map.

The General stands. Otto watches him shade his eyes with his hand and peers in the same direction, through binoculars. Something shaking that might be the skeleton of a tree, an outcrop of low green scrub such as you get on this godforsaken plain. But the General appears to be planted there: a lizard flicks across his boot. Dido nudges his shoulder but he doesn't move.

'Sir? The horses. They'll need water. They can't go on?'

At first, there is no response.

Then a laugh: a bit cracked. Sounds as if it hurt. That would be the heat and the sand in the air.

'Yes, sergeant, of course. You were right. We should have

brought camels. Did you know, you can drink camel milk?'

'Wouldn't fancy it, sir.'

'I tried it when I first met the Bedouin at Rum.'

The General has mounted Dido.

He says: 'There's water all along this route. Flaminius could be alive.'

'If you ask me, sir, he'd be better dead. For his own sake, I mean.'

'Ah, yes. For his own sake. Better dead.'

The General's face is unreadable. He pulls the scarf of his headdress across his mouth. A gift from Hatim, it is white with a gold thread, dusty now. When he first gave permission for the wearing of the kiffayah Octavius had some compunction about adopting it himself and would never consider full Arab dress. Such a masquerade would not be appreciated by the Bedouin. We are strangers and infidels, pink men from another world. At first, after their long isolation, it is possible that they saw us as savages. Perhaps we are.

Riding back to Tadmor the General points.

'There was a lake there. And trees on those hills. Panther. Gazelle.'

It is almost as if he can see them now.

They ride past the few wadis where the Bedouin still grow cotton and cereal. Nowadays, they do not go far from the city. In the midday dusk the forest of limestone looks dull, smaller.

The men who searched for Flaminius on the road to Homs have found nothing. It would have been better if they had. Even those who tormented him in life are strangely disturbed by the idea of his disappearance. The Bedouin say he is majnun – a madman possessed by jinn.

Sickness spreads among the whores. Nayra dies first, then two more. The new city is declared off limits to all but Probus and a medical assistant. It is hoped that the sponges used for contraception may have protected the men.

For three days the sky presses on the earth. Those moving below it seem reduced, crouched.

The weather will lift, Antarah will be married.

Meanwhile the General walks with Probus through the dirt streets of the new city. Mostly, the women watch him from dull eyes. One runs out to catch the corner of his cloak as he passes but he cannot understand what she says and Probus does not translate.

He says: 'She thinks you have magic powers.'

A small boy appears and others join him. They do not touch, except for one girl who is bolder and takes his hand. Probus tries to send her away but the General shakes his head.

'They break your heart,' he says. 'How are we dealing with the dead?'

Probus disapproves of the whole business of the General exposing himself to infection, to no purpose.

'It's their faith to wash them and wrap them in five white sheets, for women. Bury them facing Mecca. No coffin or headstone. But the surgeon advises cremation. We do it at night.'

'They know this?'

'We can hardly hide it from them.'

The General lingers by one doorway. Chicken are scratching in the dust. The children cluster behind him, unafraid of Probus.

In the darkness he can just make out two women crouched by a third. They are rocking on their heels and wailing.

'What are they saying?'

Probus shakes his head.

'She died without saying the words from the shahada – the prayer every Moslem should say, the last words before death.'

Probus is anxious to get on. The children would follow but are turned back by the guards.

The General's face is closed.

'Do we know what the disease is?'

'Could have been from the Savages, sir, but you'd think that would have come out before. The captain-surgeon's baffled. He says the men are clear of venereal disease – except for Flaminius and he hasn't been near the women.'

'What do you think, Probus? You know them better than the surgeon.'

Probus hesitates.

'I think it's suicide, sir. What I mean is, they say the mind rules the body. So if it can cure it can also destroy. It wouldn't be conscious, but they might have willed themselves to die. They see themselves as dishonoured and cursed in a way we can hardly understand. The queer thing is, the children dying too.'

The General nods. When he does speak his expression is impassive.

'I am ashamed.'

A Bedouin woman passes them, carrying a lamb. She averts her head and spits, but not before they notice that her face is smeared with coloured paste.

The spitting is against the evil eye, the paste to avert bad spirits.

'Even when Hatim was alive they had begun to go back to the old gods but I've never seen that before.'

Octavius remembers. 'When I was in Egypt there was a woman who had no son. She went to the temple at night to pray to Amun. She got her son but he was born club-footed.'

They have reached the northern gate to the encampment. The guard salutes.

Probus wonders. 'That might explain the Blue Warriors, the Savages – some sort of paste.'

The General seems not to have heard him. He has a strange look about him, a waxy pallor.

Conditioning and long habit, as well as disposition, make it impossible for Probus to cross the line as Severus does, in his relationship with the General. There is mutual respect and trust. Ironically, as professionals, Probus has more in common with Octavius than does Severus. But it is a mutuality not intimacy.

'How do you judge the mood of the Bedouin, Probus?'

'Dangerous. The preparations for the wedding will help. But Antarah has no real control. Jafnah's coming for the wedding. Maybe he can pull them together.'

'Go and see Antarah, lieutenant. Try to persuade him the women are no threat.'

'Sir.'

Probus does not like to say: you should go, speak chief to chief.

There is something about his gaze. What can he see?

At his tent the General says: 'I was happy at Keraq, Probus, and I didn't know it. Were you?'

'I don't think much about happiness, sir.'

The General is the heart and the brains of the encampment, of this society that he has imagined into being. If the General is sick, so, accordingly, is the garrison.

Octavius lies in his tent. He has a low fever but does not sweat. He sends away his servant. He is possessed by two images, imaginings. The dark act within himself so clearly realised that he recognises, with horror, the few fatal steps that lie between imagination and conduct. He has taken them.

And then the fever rises. He sweats, dozes, and wakes possessed by the lost paradise in the desert. He turns his whole will from the fear of himself to this vision. It shines like redemption.

There is always a murmur from the Valley of Tombs but now the air is full of voices. Antarah raging against Manah because she wears the red skirt of the married woman. The men grumbling in the barracks. The wailing of the whores from the new city.

A stalk-like shape forms out of the dirty light and then others. There is a crack of gunfire, a greeting answered from the Bedouin camp, and Jafnah, the uncle of Antarah, rides in.

In the desert Flaminius hears and sees. Or, since he feels no more pain, it might be his lingering spirit that gazes from the rings of bone his eye-sockets have become and, as he sheds the last of the cloths that bind him, shapes his mouth into a round O of wonder or fear. Or it might be surprise.

12

My darling, I dreamed last night that you were dead. I woke in tears. But women, even in the happiest of circumstances, have such dreams. Paulina tugged me back to reality, impatient to begin the day, and I was thankful. She wears me out often but she keeps me pegged to the ordinary, small things of life.

It was laundry day so I went to the stream with Mary and Anne. Paulina played naked in the stream in seventh heaven while we beat the sheets with stones. I suddenly remembered watching the fellahin women on the Nile and thinking what hard lives they had. So they do. But now I can understand the mysteries and pleasures of women working and talking together. There is something very old about this, like a rite rehearsed while its origins have been long forgotten.

It is the same working at the loom or sewing in the evening by lantern-light or candle. We talk and in talking and sewing it is as though we were sewing our dreams and memories. We do not speak much of our hopes because we dare not, but in lengthening a child's dress, patching a trouser-knee, we are celebrating, commemorating; and as we stitch we have an illusion, at least, of control. I daresay in the web we weave around ourselves for those few hours, shadows too are caught in the fabric of our work, griefs and losses. There are enough of those. Anne brought with her a precious supply of wonderful embroidery silks. We use those sparingly, like spending gold, for smocking, and then it is a festival.

You remember, I used to find Penelope at her loom too

patient, spinning and weaving the years away? Now I understand.

Sometimes, my love, I think that, in spite of its hardships, this is not a bad life. I imagine that you and I have chosen to live like this. But the fancy doesn't last. It might suit you very well. Not me. I need some bustle, the world, books, music.

. . . I wrote that last night. Today Anne's husband has arrived after a dangerous journey from Tivoli. He says that Tivoli is so consumed by rivalries, dissension, that it looks only inward. They have forgotten their place in the world, the frontiers, the empire. It is a village now, ruled by soothsayers, fortune-tellers, charlatans, murderous feuds. Lucius Tarquinius will not get out of bed until he has his horoscope! He has his personal reader of dreams and is obsessed by imagined fears for his health. So when he receives someone they must approach no closer than fifteen feet, no one must touch his hand and he has a taster for his food and drink.

The newcomer says too that there are many rumours of plots against Lucius Tarquinius. The Military Command is said to be involved. There is talk of a new Emperor. He says your name has been mentioned! I can imagine how you would laugh if you knew that. You'd make a good Emperor, I think, but the most reluctant one ever crowned.

Oh, my love, I know you can't hear this, you may never even read it. I will not allow myself to contemplate the future. My best comfort is that you are far away from Tivoli and perhaps safer so.

I have never in my life before been so conscious of the consolation of small matters. Watching Paulina frown as she puzzles out a word in her reading lesson. The taste of a pear from our own orchard.

Horace said something about that, I remember, about his little farm. One of the Odes. A family salt-cellar shining on a modest table. The soul content with the present not fearing the future.

I wish I could feel that. I can't, not altogether, and I don't believe Horace did either. I have to fight my will all the time. But at least I have learned a little about living in the present. So even though my faith is uncertain, I go to the chapel, take communion, accept the beauty of the singing and the candle-flame on the altar-table, the heads bowed, Jerome's prayers. And there, down in this cellar-sanctuary, our secret place, I close my eyes the better to hear those sweet voices.

Then for a while I can forget this strange feeling I have that you are in a new danger of some kind, something that comes between us. There is a silence, a shadow, as if I were standing in the sun and you were in the dark.

13

'So what do you think, Severus?'

'I think I'll take your pawn, sir.'

Octavius has sweated out his fever. He and the lieutenant are playing chess in the General's tent.

Octavius is better but to Severus he looks gaunt. The cords on his neck stand out. There are dark smudges under his eyes. Normally they are well matched at chess. Severus is the quick, intuitive player, Octavius slower but more thoughtful and less likely to make a dangerous move. Tonight, however, he has lost his queen in the first fifteen minutes.

He leans back and puts his hand to his neck.

Last night something extraordinary happened. Not until dawn did the guards see that the women had left the new city. Only the dead remained. Search parties found nothing. The desert had swallowed them.

'It is a terrible thing. Why do you suppose they went?'

Severus shakes his head.

'Even Probus can't explain it. The surgeon thinks the disease may have reached their brains, sent them mad. It was your order to burn the new city, sir?'

Octavius nods.

'The surgeon advised it. And the Bedouin will be satisfied. If only we could burn all our mistakes.'

'It was not a mistake at the time, sir.'

Severus watches Octavius touch his bishop and then change his mind. In a flick of vision he sees something suffering about his patience.

'You know the meanings of Tadmor, Severus? No one can be certain but there are three possible derivations. There is to protect, and to cover or bury. And there is destruction. All three make sense, don't they?'

Octavius makes his move, at first glance well-judged; but Severus can see two moves ahead when the General's bishop will be perilously exposed. He has left himself no flexibility.

He fills their glasses.

'Without the women we can expect trouble from the men. You remember Tacitus, Severus? The mutiny at Pannonia. Then Germany. The soldiers grown to old men on barbarian frontiers. I could never manage the Latin, hardly anyone could. But I do remember the history. A good writer, sharp. He saw the end of things.'

'That's how you see it now, sir?'

'It is a parallel hard to avoid.'

The General has emptied his glass and filled it again. He is in no way drunk but he is drinking the wine as though it were necessary to him, almost indifferently, as you might swallow a glass of water.

Severus has been thinking. He speaks tentatively.

'If you were to declare yourself Emperor? I think the men would rally to you. I don't mean to march on Tivoli. But to give their presence here a meaning, to unite them with you, rather than against you?'

'And tell me, Severus, what would the King of Tadmor do for his next trick? Turn the desert to water or wine?'

'Yes, sir. I do see.'

In three moves Severus reaches checkmate.

They sit on, drinking, Octavius more than Severus.

What is in his head, behind those dazed eyes? Is it wine or the lassitude after fever? Severus feels he must sit out his silence. And so he drinks. And so he sees the heaviness, the weariness of the General in the attitude of his wide shoulders.

'What ideas we had in the old days, didn't we, Severus. We never did restore the Temple of the Signa. An impossible project.'

Severus's head droops.

The General is saying: 'I shall speak to Jafnah about the Savages. I don't trust him as I did Hatim but he would be more use than Antarah. I shall make a decision after the wedding.'

'Sir.'

'You must turn in. Thank you for your company.'

As the lieutenant is about to stand Octavius speaks again.

'I remember a lost palace in the desert. Or it might have been a city.'

In his quarters Severus is glad to find Ali. The boy has fallen asleep naked waiting for him. In sleep he is beautiful: the defenceless buttocks, the curve of the spine. Severus undresses and blows out the lamp. The air has lifted. It is nearly dawn.

'How many times, Ali, have I told you to wash your feet before you come to bed.'

Now the sky has cleared there is a chill in the air. Severus is thankful for the warmth of flesh, any flesh.

Only when his head touches the pillow does he realise how exhausted he is.

'I can't make love tonight, Ali. But I'll pay you all the same.'

Perhaps the boy does understand. He turns and smiles and opens his arms and, cradled by the child, Severus sleeps.

In spite of the wine Octavius does not sleep, nor does he feel the need.

Through the last few days his army log has been neglected. He brings it up to date. Sortie into desert after deserter. Search for the women. Other facts. He keeps this log as he always did. He hardly pauses to reflect that no one may ever read it, or if they do, it will be after his death. This is simply an unquestioned duty of his years in command.

Not for the first time he sees himself as the captain of a vessel, having set out cheerfully enough on a voyage; doomed now to sail on a nail-sick ship in dangerous waters with little hope of home. If, in the wreck of Tadmor his log is found, it will be scrupulously correct. Wryly, he thinks, Gaius Germanicus would approve.

It is the General who keeps the log. The journal, kept by the man, is the story of quite another voyage: that of a husband, a son, a father, a child, a soul. A man who would not be Emperor. A husband who had an idiotic fancy that in writing here he could speak to his wife.

Now even if you could hear me, Livia, I would not speak. What I have to write down because I feel compelled, would worry and bewilder you. The General continues to function but I am stumbling in some kind of bleak country where even a compass would serve no purpose. I have lost my magnetic north. There is no right way clear . . . Everywhere I go I see the sway of a red skirt at the corner of my vision. And then there is a sight of green promising an oasis, a palace, an uncharted city . . . the dream of courts and gardens and fountains. I heard of it once but cannot find it in the maps or the books. I have the feeling, if I can reach this place it might save me.

I think, of all the people in my life, only Pausonias would have understood my predicament and would not call me mad. Though, in a world he considered ridiculous he would mock my sense of sin.

I used to say that I was a simple man. Now I know, I am simply a man.

There will be the wedding but first there is a queer kind of mourning.

The General seems to have possession of himself again. He gives orders for wedding gifts, for extra beer for the barracks to celebrate the wedding. There is little left to give to Antarah so Octavius orders his servant to empty his own cedar chest, inlaid with ebony and mother-of-pearl from the Indian Ocean, and a few coins from the last of their gold. A silk robe he had bought to take home to Tivoli for Livia.

But the Bedouin will have no wedding while there remains even a trace of ill omen. So first, Octavius must witness the burning of the new city. It is his duty. It must be done by day and Otto and Probus must attend him.

As the new city burns there is a wailing, anululation.

'What's that, Probus?'

'The Bedouin women, sir. In spite of everything, they are mourning for the whores because they died in sin. They believe they were possessed by jinn. Well, that's how they see it.'

Just as they have waited for a breeze to blow the sparks away from Tadmor, so the same light wind carries the queer trilling from the women who, against the light, are the colour of ash.

The kindling was dry. There had been no need to use precious fuel. But there is something else. It was Otto who had said that there should be some kind of prayer. He had come last night to the General's tent.

The General was inclined to smile but had taken the sergeant seriously.

'I thought you had nothing to do with superstition, Otto?'

The sergeant was clearly uncomfortable.

'I don't, sir. It's decency. Perhaps you could say a word.'

'Ah. The word. Well. I wish. I have none for this, Otto. We must ask Lieutenant Probus. He knows their ways.'

Probus has no idea what to say.

'It might be tactless to ask the Bedouin, sir. So I found something in the Koran.'

'Carry on.'

Probus steps forward. It is an odd little ceremony. He speaks to the fire the words he has written down.

'Rejoice this day. You shall enter gardens watered by

running streams in which you shall abide for ever.'

He stands back.

'I think there's a prayer for children but I can't find it.'

'That will do very well, lieutenant.'

Otto's face is set. He watches a rag lifted and carried by the breeze and the fire. He has never in his life felt like this and the words are locked in him.

I don't know how to say it, what I feel. Something a bit crazy. Nayra and the children, I keep thinking about them, can't get my mind off it. She was a steady woman. There was something kind and good about her even after all she'd gone through. At first I just used her as I've used any whore or willing woman all these years. Then I suppose she was a sort of home.

She died when I was in the desert with the General. I was numb. I just got on with things as usual. But now it's more like anger. Maybe this is what men feel while women cry?

I don't trust myself. It's as if those demons the Bedouin go on about had got me.

Otto is the last to turn away and leave the fire. Not that the new city can ever be entirely burned or wiped from the earth. Traces remain for ever.

So Octavius reflects as he looks back. Then he walks on beside Probus. In the fresher weather and clearer light the old city is golden again. He observes this but today the beauty of the place does not touch him.

Probus says: 'I think the men are blaming the Bedouin, sir, for what happened to the women.'

'That's absurd. But I see it. I leave it to you, Probus. You know what I've been thinking, lieutenant? If the Savages came I'd be thankful. There is a lot to be said for an enemy you can see.'

A boy shakes a tambourine, another joins in with the one-stringed instrument – goatskin on a wooden frame – which sings with a weird, poignant sound, something like a plaintive threnody in all the rejoicing.

The wedding preliminaries and celebration will go on for seven days. They have barely begun. While in her tent the women paint the bride's hands and feet with henna, the men drink coffee.

In appearance, Jafnah and his clan are marked out from the Bedouin of Tadmor by a leanness verging on emaciation. Octavius has noticed before the difference between the desert nomads and the settled, admired the way the former will ride all day without food and when they do eat and drink they do so sparingly. Like Jafnah, they are not sick but honed.

Jafnah rises as the General approaches. They embrace as equals. It is Jafnah not Antarah who calls for more coffee.

When the courtesies are done Octavius settles on the rug between Jafnah and Antarah, Probus at his shoulder. The old nomad, with his hook nose and carved cheeks, has hardly changed; though Octavius notices that the glaucoma is spreading to the other eye. Probus translates as each speaks, stumbling occasionally at Jafnah's Arabic, less pure than was Hatim's.

There is polite talk of the wedding to come. Young Antarah still strikes Octavius as a little stiff and solemn. He seems uncomfortable in the presence of his uncle. Probus has heard that there is trouble between Antarah and his sister Manah, who has refused to take the husband of his choice.

While Antarah remains stern-faced Jafnah laughs often, showing yellow fangs, his only remaining teeth; his eyes, even though misted, dart from face to face. He smells. He would be capable of duplicity for its own sake, Octavius guesses, as a game. And yet it is impossible not to warm to him.

He wags his unkempt beard.

'I see that in the years since we met the General has learned the wisdom of a grandfather.'

Octavius shakes his head.

'How is that?'

'His hair is grey, which is the colour of understanding.' Jafnah laughs like a dog. 'When it is white like my beard he will have knowledge of all things that Allah permits. My nephew here is not master of his own sister.'

There is a sharp intake of breath from Antarah. Around them there is constant coming and going, the shuffle of camels, singing, shouts of greeting or temper. Since Jafnah's arrival the encampment has doubled in size.

Octavius is embarrassed but Jafnah, having caused a crackle of tension, goes on, his face now drawn into severity, or a clowning of seriousness.

'My nephew has the name of a great poet of the Days of Ignorance. May he be the greatest of all fathers and chiefs, by the grace of Allah. When his family too were true Bedouin there were many raids even between our two kin.'

'You can't remember those days, Jafnah?' Octavius smiles.

Jafnah shrugs. He is abruptly, fleetingly, bored.

'It is remembered.' Now his face closes in melancholy. Through the years Octavius has learned to recognise and to be patient with these sudden plunges into despair. He is tired himself, immeasurably tired. His neck aches. He would like to leave this body behind, step from his flesh, sloughing off its relict in these dreary sands; then he would become air and light. In Livia's sense he has no faith. Yet in Tadmor over the years Octavius, the man of reason, has imagined he could see the winds of eternity in the dazzle of summer stars.

'And now?'

Jafnah's voice is hoarse.

'We are the last tribe and we have no home in the desert.'

'Jafnah, I need a man, a guide, who knows this country as you do. Where would I find such a man?'

'Aah.' Jafnah lets out a sigh. Negotiations with the nomad would always be more complicated than they were with Hatim. He enjoys games.

He wags his head. 'Who is left who knows the ways? Where is there a well unpoisoned?'

'There would be gifts, of course.'

That shrug again.

'What use are the finest of presents to a dead man?'

'Gold.'

Probus translates but he is startled. The General has given in too soon. Anyone else might have earned Jafnah's contempt. And Probus knows they are down to the last of their gold. Besides, where can he lead them? Without fuel, a foray to the desert is out of the question.

Sweetmeats are brought round. Imru grabs greedily. There is talk of the earthquake and the weather, Antarah's hopes for his crops.

Octavius nods but he seems distracted. He turns to Jafnah again.

'Tell me, have you heard of a city in the desert? An oasis. A place of gardens and fountains? A palace?'

'The General surely speaks of the Garden of Eden. That does not belong to you Christians alone. For Syrians that is Damascus.' Jafnah spreads his hands, the gesture of the story-teller. 'God made Adam from the clay of the Barada river. It was a city of trees and fountains. Rose-water. Apricots.'

'No. Not Damascus.'

'There.' Jafnah points to the north-east. 'There was Qasr el-Hair. The palace of Caliph Hisham.'

'No. It is a place not in the books, only in stories.'

The intensity of the General's questioning puzzles Probus. Jafnah's interest appears to flicker. He lacks Hatim's gentle courtesy. There is a distraction. A band of women, brightly dressed, shouting and laughing, ululating outside the bride's tent. The sound of clapping. A rifle fired. Camels bellowing in perpetual complaint. A small girl carrying a puppy stands round-eyed, gazing at the men. Octavius glances up and there is Manah, the child by the stream in spring, the lost daughter. Years and years ago. Octavius feels dizzy. Antarah shouts at the child, chasing her away.

Octavius rubs his hand across his eyes.
'Come on, Probus.'
He is about to stand when Jafnah catches his sleeve.
'I might know of a place where men take their sorrows.'

I am alternately shivering and in a sweat. This may be a return of the malaria I had in Africa but it feels more like a sickness of the spirit.

You can't hear me, Livia, no one can. My head is a sounding-box.

Severus watches me. His touch with the oils on my aching neck was almost tender last night. I can't believe that I allowed myself even to imagine a giving-way to that particular temptation. Not that I regard the Greek way as sinful: it is simply something my flesh would find repugnant. And my duty here would not permit such intimacy. Perhaps I have already gone too far? The truth is, Severus's presence has consoled me for the loss of Rufus.

I wonder, my love, is there an act of darkness in all of us, just as there is the possibility of courage and love?

Do women know this as a matter of course? I think so.

Severus says Otto has been drinking since the wedding celebrations began. Steady, sturdy Otto.

For seven days they sing and dance. The sheep's throat is cut at the entrance to the bridal tent. The blood runs out.

Seven years we have been here. Most of the time a competent adjutant could command this garrison.

I have begun to worry about the possibility of an attack from Tivoli by air or land. I look up at the mountains, those beautiful folds of rock falling away where the Anti-Lebanon brushes the desert. Those peaks will be snow-capped soon.

Winter comes early here. I cannot imagine Tivoli – except for that small place we had together as husband and wife, our bed, autumn, the heavy fruit, the scent of the first olive-wood fire of the season. The ilex grove where we met by the bottomless pool. I can see us so young then. I was awkward, afraid to speak to you. But you already had that open, clear gaze, kind eyes, bright with intelligence.

I would never have dreamed I would love your age even more than your youth, but there was something triumphant, wasn't there, about our middle-aged passion. The strange thing is, since my mind has been in turmoil, I see us from such a great distance: the room, the bed, the two lovers, grow smaller until I am afraid I shan't see them any more. I feel like a man craning to find Arcturus in the summer sky, from which to map the heavens. Severus showed me how to follow the curve of the Plough's handle. From there we found the Northern Crown just east of Boötes. And to the south and east, red Antares.

One late summer years ago, Severus and I took mats out into the desert away from the lights of the encampment to spend the night voyaging among the stars. And it was a voyage we made, lying on our backs, through the ocean of the Milky Way, nearly overhead, spotting the landmarks of the Northern Cross, the Lyre and the Eagle. We were so dazzled he told me to close my eyes and then we opened them and I followed him to the Archer, the Dolphin and the Arrow.

I shall never forget that night. Yet it seems set in crystal, as distant a vision as that of the two rich lovers celebrating our marriage as if we had conquered a great city.

In this expanding universe those stars that look nailed to the black sky are like the two of us in each other's arms, apotheosised, spinning away at speeds we cannot imagine.

To most of the western ears the Bedouin music is at its best plaintive. To Otto it sounds like the screaming of cats on heat.

But he stays, tipsy, red-eyed, squatting by himself, mesmerised by the clapping and the rhythm of the feast.

The flame leaps, putting out the stars. An older woman dances. There are mounds of rice and mutton and goat.

I wouldn't care if I never saw another bloody Bedouin, another grain of sand.

Yes, you're right: Otto's pissed. They've got some home-made stuff in the barracks, stronger than beer. These gypsies the General's so keen on don't need booze. They get crazy on the racket they're making.

The men are confined to the garrison while the wedding's on but there's been a few each night slipped out in the dark. I've turned a blind eye.

There's that goat-girl, Antarah's sister Manah, dancing with the rest now her brother's in the wedding tent. I tell you, a spot of that cunt and I'd get myself straight in the head again.

I'm drinking to get Nayra out of my mind. And the other women and the children. And stuff that goes further back, that I don't think of in my right mind. I mean, my own woman, the kids, home. When you're a regular you can't dwell on that. You think of it sometimes, that's natural but thinking's not good now. I reckon there's no home to go to.

The trouble with booze, it doesn't stop you dreaming. Last night I smelled green fields after rain.

Don't worry about Otto. I'll get right. Sober up. Carry on. Do my duty even in this arsehole in the sand. Stand by the General.

Gives you a balls-ache though.

The last day and night of the wedding feast. I have put in appearances, with Probus.

I have been thinking, Livia, about your Christians. I was brought up to believe in the new Roman ethic, that there is only crime and punishment. On this point, for once,

Pausonias and Gaius Germanicus were in agreement.

Now I wonder about your people. I used to find the Christian preoccupation with sin absurdly morbid. The cross struck me as a barbaric symbol. It still does. I hate the sight of it here, ragged against the evening light, and have considered ordering that it be taken down.

You showed me the words for Christian baptism when we were planning before she was born to have Paulina christened, and I was repelled then by the notion of original sin. What could be more innocent than a new-born child?

Lately, since I have lost my way, I am coming, I think, to a different view. I can't accept the existence of the devil or the idea of a godparent putting away the fiend on behalf of an infant. But it does seem likely that we are born with fiend and angel in us, with the capacity for great good and great evil.

Many of us, the drones like me, pass our lives on a middle plain, doing little harm and little good.

But that has altered.

Since the earthquake.

I'm glad you can't hear me. This sounds like madness.

Words escape me. Flick away like moths.

I function as Commander of the garrison. Perhaps Severus suspects. No one else.

I am sometimes caught by a nostalgia for our early days in Tadmor so sharp I could be calling out for the childhood I never had.

The rising beat of the wedding, the wild music that goes on through half the night, keep me awake, draw me and repel me. A barbarian shout it is, under a black sky. I pull on my cloak. My hands are shaking almost too much to fasten the buckle.

I envy you and your Christians the consolation of penitence and redemption.

Salvation is a glorious word.

14

See the General in the sloping light of late summer. Short-legged like Odysseus, strong-shouldered, he paces the hectares of Tadmor. He has always had a stillness of presence, so he seems taller than he is. All the same, seen from a distance, Tadmor dwarfs him, as it reduces any man, by its great age, its indifference, its vastness.

This last changes according to the light: so at a certain season and time of day and aspect of the sun, standing in the bows of the great hulk of the Bel Temple, by turning his head a man imagines that with a single gaze he can encompass the whole site. But then the fingering of light and shade shifts and the gazer blinks, confused.

There is something alarming about the way even a company of men can be swallowed and lost to sight. The human voice is too puny to carry across this immensity of ruins.

Sometimes, alone, he rides Dido further than is prudent into the desert, to the east and south, where the horizon is an ever-shaking mirage, a topographical insanity; as you think you are nearing it, it dissolves and retreats. Octavius is drawn to ride on, as though that dangerous, shimmering heat might swallow him and transform him to radiance. And at the moment he is taken back into the matter of the universe, he will hear an answer. Or he will know what the question is.

In his reason, Octavius says to himself that he has committed an unforgivable act; and his punishment may be that there can be no absolution for him because he cannot ask or expect forgiveness; he has no god to pray to, no priest to shrive him. As for Manah, whenever she comes to his mind, she is the child by the stream to whom, in spring, he gave the eagle brooch.

So he sentences himself to carry his transgression within himself, a stone or a thorn, lodged quietly in his flesh.

Dido stumbles. She is not so young. She was covered once, by Hatim's only remaining stallion, but the foal died in being born. Hatim advised that a second attempt might kill her.

She jerks up her head and sidesteps a heaped cairn of stones – a scorpion perhaps. The mare has a good instinct for such dangers.

Octavius responds. He has ridden too far. He scans the desert that has become, along with the city, the landscape of his soul. It is a terrible place, this country of the Savages. Yet he has dreamed of the lost garden contained there.

Not long ago they found the bones of the women strewn here. Not strewn – arranged in a purposeful bier, with cold ashes beneath. Octavius has taken fate of the women on himself. Their deaths, together with his guilt and the conviction that Tivoli will send an assault force against him, have become part of a flickering madness. The Savages too: he imagines he has seen them out here, mounted on creatures that were neither camels nor horses, he has smelled them on the wind and turned his head to glimpse them on the uncertain horizon, watching him. They were the colour of sand, not indigo.

Perhaps this is not a fantasy: a force from Tivoli may be in the mountains, the Savages in the desert.

Octavius shakes his head. Riding back into Tadmor, there is the comfortable scent of roasting coffee beans, the camels' groan. The Bedouin encampment has doubled in size. Jafnah shows no sign of taking his people away. There is trouble among the black tents. The last of the olives have been picked. The air is fresher, the light steadier.

Is that Manah over there, with her goats?

Several times Octavius has found mysterious gifts left just inside his tent or by his pillow. Olives wrapped in vine leaves.

A few figs or dates. He asked no one about them nor could he bring himself to eat them. He goes to Antarah's hearth only at night and is careful to stay within the circle of men. It is necessary to visit the Bedouin. Courtesy demands it. And Jafnah himself is to guide the expedition into the desert.

The men do not notice that the General is in any way troubled. His manner has always been a little stiff.

Besides, he is meticulous as ever in the observation of his duty. Wryly, he thinks, at least I have the appearance of *honestas*. Manly courage, reputation.

Have I got it right this time, Gaius Germanicus? And the lead seal of the imaginary Emperor, that is *honos*? Something bestowed. Appropriate that it should be cast in a base metal.

So even though, as Severus fears, the man may be sick or troubled, the General is in his tent. He is seen to be there. He takes daily reports, plans the expedition. He nods, makes notes, gives orders. He appears weary but alert.

When Probus has left, Octavius leans back in his chair. The tent flap is open and in the low light he sees particles dancing in the sunbeam, remembers Lucretius and his turbulent atoms. Radiance is composed of atoms linked and massed together. Harmony is an illusion. Unless turbulence has its own hidden order.

Octavius hears the stamp of men drilling. Voices carry in the clearer air. The sound of wagon-wheels over stone; a shout; the smells: men, beasts, iron, smoke. How he had loved all this, in Asia, in Arabia, in Africa, it had been as much his home as Livia's hearth. More.

In this command, in Tadmor, he had relished the sensation that in this settlement of his invention, his imagination, there was a true symbiosis. So many connections of nerve and tissue making up a whole.

But he no longer feels this. He is disconnected.

Only alone and unresisted is the atom free to follow a fixed course.

You see, Gaius Germanicus, I remembered something.

The sun leaves coins of gold on my table. In Tivoli the leaves will be crisping. They hang like that, frozen, until a gale rattles them from the tree.

The garrison is full of rumours, fear of winter, wild talk. The General has doubled defences in the lower slopes of the mountains.

Octavius spends his nights in his new winter quarters in the Arab castle. From here he has a clear view of the Valley of Tombs. He walks there still but the voices have fallen silent or he cannot hear them.

He sends for Severus.

Meanwhile he makes up the army log and his personal journal, though it is no longer clear where one ends and the other begins. It doesn't matter. In the event of assault or action he has decided to burn both.

He writes.

Probus reports two desertions. He is worried. A man I remember as a boy seven years ago, Publius, is inciting mutiny. It's the loss of the women and the fear of winter. Since it is hard to imagine what form mutiny could take – except for my death – the consensus, so far as there is one, is for mass desertion before snow closes the mountain route.

Publius would be the same age as Rufus. He has red hair. I remember him playing football that first spring.

I remember.

'Severus, come and sit by the fire.'

Octavius has the maps spread on his table. By day the room in the Arab castle is dark, with only a slit for a window. At night it resembles a large cave more than a room. A rudimentary chimney has been cut and a wood-fire lit. The light from the flames does not reach the further shadows but it flicks the faces of the General and the lieutenant.

Octavius smiles.

'You see my new rug? A present from Antarah. Did you

know, those four outer stars stand for Mecca, prayer, Ramadan and the Koran? And in the centre, charity.' Octavius fills their wine glasses.

'I learned early – it's easy to romanticise the Bedouin. We must not make that mistake. Probus believes we should trust neither Jafnah nor Imru. Poor Probus. So serious.'

'Perhaps he has reason to be. We all have.'

The General tips back his head so that his face is lost.

'You too, Severus?'

'Sir, there are real dangers. You shouldn't ride alone in the desert. You should not move even within the camp without a guard.'

There is the glitter in Octavius's eyes.

'The day I need guarding against my own men, I wouldn't wish to live.'

His throat sounds dry as if he had a thirst that could never be slaked.

'I've been thinking of that night we spent under the stars, Severus. You told me their names. It was like a voyage.'

Severus thinks: there is something unearthly about him. He is like a shaman who has died and returned. If I touched his hand it would be cold.

If I could warm him.

Octavius says: 'We were talking about Tacitus, the mutiny at Pannonia. I looked it up. Old men mutilated by wounds serving their fortieth year. In sight of savages. We use that word too easily and never about ourselves. Who is to say that their empire would be any worse than ours? It could be that we've had our day.'

There is the clatter of the guard changing outside. Above their heads is the watchtower. This place is an eyrie, valuable for its vantage but ominous. The castle seems to have no connection with the city. It has the air of a brutal afterthought.

'I don't count my life for much, Severus.' The shadows are heaped against their backs. 'I used to think how convenient it would be if a man's life might keep pace with history. Dawn, noon and dark. Perhaps for me, it has.'

Severus senses that for the moment the General has put aside his rank. He can speak frankly.

'Should we let those men who want to, try for home? Before winter?'

'And where is home?' The fire smokes. Severus's eyes prick. Octavius seems lost in thought. What shapes does he see in those flames? 'I have my duty to them as they have to me. I have broken one trust. That is enough.'

The General appears to have forgotten Severus's presence. Then he looks up. His tone is calm.

'If I'm no longer here. If I were sick, perhaps, you and Probus will share the command. In matters of strategy, you must defer to him. And both of you can rely on Otto.' He stands and goes to the table. 'I have put this in writing, here somewhere. For what it's worth I've stamped it with the Emperor's seal. The men might be swayed by that. Now, bring the lamp. You see, here, I've marked the route.'

The General uses the dividers to indicate. 'Jafnah says the Savages are at Dayr az Zawr. I think they are closer.' Octavius pricks the map again. To Severus this whole area looks like a terrible emptiness. 'And there in that quarter might be the lost place we are looking for.'

For the first time, Severus wonders if the General might be mad.

They sit on by the fire and Octavius speaks of the pleasure-castle of Yezid, the second Ommayad Caliph. He has lost his tiredness. He is calling up towers and minarets, courtyards and fountains.

'But you must come with me to Jafnah. He remembers it, though he has never seen it.'

Severus waits out half the night with the General. The servant brings food and more wine, makes up the fire. He sets the chessboard between the two men but tonight there will be no game.

Octavius says: 'I'm glad to have your company. I'm not sleeping so well.'

He asks if Severus is tired.

He talks, entirely rationally, about Tivoli: the swimming-pond, the Academy, his son.

'We've begun to think that Tadmor is the whole world, haven't we? Tell me, Severus, what you hoped for when you came.'

'What I found.'

'Tadmor?'

'Yes.'

The General's tone is almost gentle.

'You are not under orders, lieutenant, for this expedition.'

But he knows he will follow this man anywhere. *We shall go, we shall go, whenever you lead the way*.

'You remember I said I had no ideas, Severus? I think I have become what my tutor called a dog-soldier. Ideas are fleas, he said, and fleas need dogs. After all, I am a dog with fleas.'

Back in his quarters, Severus finds Ali asleep on the mat. He has not the heart to wake the boy.

He studies the paper the General gave him. It is a precisely written order beneath the heading: in case of my death.

The document makes perfect sense. The seal is there. Above it, the signature is a scrawl, wandering, as though written by a blind man.

In the night there is a wind from the north, a forerunner of winter.

Standing by Otto's brazier outside the castle, Octavius remembers how at this time of year, even on a windless day, a breeze always ruffled the surface of the bottomless pool at Tivoli, as if it had its own weather.

Time in youth, in those days, felt infinite, boundless. Now

it passes in a blink; so yesterday you were diving under the ilex, and then you break water, open your eyes and life is so short it could all have been a mirage, a trick of the light. A brief shiver and it is gone.

I sent for Publius and talked to him. He is not a mere troublemaker – it would be easier if he were – but a decent, if limited, young man. He set out his terms: immediate evacuation and return to Tivoli, or a contract limiting service, doubling pay and rations.

I told him as much of the truth as I dared: that the political situation in Tivoli means we must postpone any idea of evacuation until spring.

It's clear he holds no personal enmity for me but he was obdurate.

Finally I was obliged to say that he was risking a charge of mutiny and reminded him of the penalty. The cross hangs over us all. I can see no way out. It is abhorrent as a means of punishment and I vowed when I was first given the authority to use it, that I never would.

But if the survival of a society depends in part on prohibitions and their enforcement, then punishment for infringement must be enforced or the structure of that society is weakened. So if mutiny and treason carry the penalty of crucifixion, then the cross must stand.

I think Gaius Germanicus would approve of that proposition and conclusion. And were I to return to Tivoli, he would be one of the first to call me traitor and to demand crucifixion. And I'm not your Christ, Livia. For me there would be no redemption in such a death.

Mostly, my mind is tilted. But when something like balance is on me again, I walk about and try to talk to the men but I find it difficult.

The shadows from the mountains are lengthening. There is snow on the peaks.

The barracks have been comparatively quiet. A couple of men were caught stealing from the stores. I am most afraid that they may turn on the Bedouin. And yet I feel like a spectator not an actor. As though I had ceased to be a protagonist.

It is a month since I have seen Manah. She was by the stream and before she ran away she glanced up and her cheek was hideously bruised. She snatched her veil across her face as women do when they fear the evil eye. Probus says she has been beaten by Antarah and Imru and he has no idea what has become of her. Trying to follow her, I stumbled and fell to my knees. How I envy you, Livia. You can pray.

Last night I went with Probus and Severus to the Bedouin camp to discuss our expedition with Jafnah. The atmosphere there is strange. They have lost their cheerfulness. Antarah looks like thunder. I get the feeling that Imru is eavesdropping.

I said: 'We no longer hear the calls to prayer, Jafnah. Is there trouble with your people?'

The old nomad seemed disinclined to answer. I had been clumsy. I know they often evade the question direct.

At last he raised his face, spread his hands.

'They have abandoned Allah.' His grin was feral. 'Or Allah has abandoned them.'

That appeared to be the end of the matter so far as Jafnah was concerned. I knew better than to press. We were inside the tent. Imru squatted at the entrance, playing with one of his small sons, a baby who was going to be as fat as his father. Jafnah was running a string of amber beads through his fingers. Then suddenly he spoke, so fast and raspingly I could not catch even one word.

I turned to Probus: 'What did Jafnah say?'

Probus looked uncomfortable.

'He says they have gone back to the old goddess of the

desert, Al-Uzza. We call her the morning star. At this time of year she belongs to the evening.'

'You mean Venus, Jafnah?'

He shrugged, that eloquent twitch of the shoulders. Clearly Jafnah had no time for gods of any kind.

'She had her sanctuary of three trees close to Mecca. Mohammed himself is said to have offered to her. She asked for sacrifice.'

'What kind of sacrifice?'

'Human.'

I heard Probus draw in his breath.

I said: 'Why, Jafnah? Why do they want such a terrible god?'

'They are afraid. Of the Blue Warriors, of winter. Our grazing has gone, our wells are poisoned. I must keep my people here so there are too many of us and Antarah's men would like to drive us out. He is angry but he has no command. Men are weak. Fear makes cruel gods and savage practices. The Christians, we hear, were cannibals. They ate the body and the blood of the son of their god. What is crueller than that?'

I nodded. We talked of the expedition. I wanted to ask about Manah but I sensed that we had already asked too many questions.

Walking back to the camp I was glad of the cooler air and paused to breathe it in. I put my hand on Probus's arm. He is not one for stars and that is his strength. I was like that once or imagined myself so: content to be earthbound, measuring my destiny on this earth by the length of my pace. I slept well then. In those days my body was my friend: on campaign, in love, riding, diving, I gave it no thought, I saw no further than the end of the day.

Now my eyes are torn open. If they appear blinded, that is because they are turned inward, upon horror. If only I could keep my gaze fixed on the sky.

I said to Probus: 'Look, there she is.'

Venus hung, pendant to the crescent moon and, next to the moon, the brightest planet in the sky.

'It's hard to see her as bloodthirsty. Do you think Jafnah believes?'

'I'd say, sir, Jafnah believes in nothing he cannot touch.'

'Can he be trusted? As a guide?'

'Provided it's in his own interest. I'd hold the second part of his payment until he gets you back safely.'

We entered the city by the northern gate.

'If that's what it is.'

'You don't approve of this expedition, do you, lieutenant?'

'It is not for me to question, sir.'

Probus sounded uncomfortable. I nodded. He was right. It was folly.

I felt the greatest affection for him: his fidelity, his bewilderment, his simplicity. His simplicity most of all. How I envied him that.

'Turn in, Probus.'

I watched him go with regret and stood for a moment, getting my bearings. Vertigo is with me daily now and my eyes were star-dazzled. The moon had gone behind a cloud. A dog barked. A stone struck me on the forehead.

15

Love, I have so much to say, if you could hear. If only I could write to you or tell you!

We had news, only a month old, yesterday. The Master of Soldiers and the Military Command have risen against Lucius Tarquinius! The Praetorian Guard and some of the army appear to be with him. There have been riots but no one, at the time we heard, could be sure which way the people would go. They have suffered terribly under Lucius Tarquinius but conscription and the harsh terms of foreign service turned them against the army long ago. So the outcome's uncertain. But the rumour is, our so-called Emperor is in hiding or dead already.

This must mean the end at least of the empire and I'm not sorry about that. Imperialism and decency don't go well together, do they? But poor Tivoli. I can't help thinking. Fires every night. Villas sacked and looted. Cattle stolen and slaughtered. We are doing to ourselves what the Savages have so far failed to achieve.

And this time of year reminds me of Tivoli at her most beautiful. That golden haze, that extraordinary stillness to the trees waiting quietly for winter. I was showing Paulina how to pick apples: to watch out for wasps, beware of the reddest, weigh the apple in your hand and if it feels ready to give way, take it. Not to walk barefoot among the windfalls. Of course, she couldn't resist and got stung. She didn't cry but stuck out her bottom lip when I dabbed the place with vinegar.

We went back to our job. The kitten followed us. I watched Paulina playing with it in the deep grass and the orchard was so beautiful I found myself in tears.

And early in the morning the children go out to collect mushrooms in our fallow field. They have come through like a miracle this year. We woke one day and the field looked as though it were under snow or blossom. You can't pick without crushing some underfoot.

But I haven't told you – the messenger from Tivoli came to ask Jerome to return. You would never believe it but there is a strong movement to Christianity among the people and even some of the Senate. I thought, but didn't say, perhaps this is what happens towards the end of things, a longing for the magical? So Jerome, having taken refuge here as his namesake did in Bethlehem, is to go back as a most reluctant Pope or Archbishop or whatever they choose to call him.

Poor Jerome – he hates the idea but he'll go because he considers it his duty. Duty and faith, how I have come to detest those words! They took you from me, and Rufus, and now we are to lose a strong and gentle man who calls his goodness Christianity. I think he guessed long ago that I had lost my faith but he never spoke of it or reproached me.

I'm selfish. Perhaps when the fires die down you'll be given back to me. Even Rufus – or news of him, at least. I hardly dare hope. But whatever happens, any new order will have to pull back from the frontiers.

I've learned to avoid fanciful hope along with despair. But I have lately one waking dream I keep to myself: of peace and of exiles and tired soldiers coming home like labourers from the fields and vineyards. Women with children in their arms and at their heels. The old going back to die at their own hearths. Friends and families embracing, reunited. Even the dead on the most distant frontiers woken by those voices, rubbing their eyes and, finding themselves whole again, restored.

I didn't tell you. Gaius Germanicus was abandoned by his guards and seized by a mob. He was dragged for half a mile by a strong horse and then hanged. I can't hate him any more. I feel nothing, not even pity.

It's dark. Goodnight, my love. I kiss your eyes. Why so sad?

16

It is November, nearly winter. The Bedouin women have turned their tents to open to the lee of the wind.

There is snow on the mountain peaks. A few of the deserters have straggled back. Their poor wracked frames reproach me, as do the gaunt features of all the men. I would have said they are too near death for punishment but Probus judges otherwise and I trust him. I have to trust him because I can no longer count on my own ability to weigh a situation. My wits are astray. All my senses are set on the journey into the desert, as if whatever I find there will purge my sin. Or destroy me.

In all this I have almost forgotten Manah. Shame is selfish.

Witnessing, as I was obliged to do, the flogging of the man who flung the harmless pebble at me out of the dark, I envied him his punishment.

Probus reminded me that I am not free. I am myself and at the same time the symbol, the emblem of authority.

I was sitting by the fire, my hands as empty as my eyes. I tried to set him at his ease but he was still uncomfortable. I told him to take wine, to join me at the hearth, to say what he had to say.

When he had finished I nodded. I hoped he didn't notice that my hand shook as I reached for the flask of wine.

'You are recalling me to my duty, lieutenant. Thank you.'

'Sir. I wish—'

I cut him off.

'You have been the best of my men, Probus. You might say you are the best of myself.'

* * *

Oh, Livia, I am drunk. You've never seen that, have you? A skinful of wine, pissed as a common soldier.

Probus is right about the deserters. And the men. I had known it myself but I hid, like a child under the bedclothes, its ears covered.

The General shall do his duty.

And Probus knows about Manah, I'm sure now. He must have seen her after that night, by my tent. My worst punishment may be that I can do nothing for her. We cannot interfere with Bedouin justice. She can't have named me.

I don't know how I got to the stables in the dark but here I am. No one else. Just a lamp. The smell of horse and dust and leather and my Dido, queen of Arabia, tosses her head, snorting at my drunkenness.

Have I told you what a wonder she is? When he gave her to me Hatim explained, under that white coat she wears a second, dark skin. He called it the keheilan. It protects her from the sun.

I wanted to ask Probus: do they know that the General is mad? That all they have is the shell of office, a husk as dry as the chaff I rub between my fingers?

Dido, why are you kind to me, this reeling man, muzzling my shoulder as I rest my face against your neck?

Look, you see, the design of this creature is very precise. The large, wide-set dark eyes give her a greater field of vision. Even more remarkably, five rather than six lumbar vertebrae mean she can wheel in the tightest circle. You have seen her captive sisters on display at the Villa d'Este. Their arched tails carried high, their flared nostrils that close like a camel's in sandstorms.

And greatest wonder of all: that delicate muzzle so small she can drink from a pot or a cupped hand.

Hatim told me God made this horse from the south wind.

The Bedouin say she can fly without wings.

Tired. Let go. The wine pulls me down. Was that you that laughed, Pausonias? The drunken general – what do you make of that? I could never decide if you were all-sceptical or all-forgiving.

Rest. Might sleep for a change. Hatim, I miss you. Will you be waiting there, in the desert, a sandman, a jinn? Your spirit. That couldn't be put out.

Queen Dido, why are you shouting?

Just as well it was me that found him. Otto. Heard that precious horse of his and there he was, passed out. The lamp knocked over. The flame just caught the straw. Flung water from the trough and trampled it with my cloak. Pretty mess.

So, I'll tell you: chucked some water over him too. Opened those queer eyes at me and I heaved him up. He's not tall but heavier than you'd think.

The night air hit him and he sagged. But then he got his legs, more or less, and there was a cloud over the moon, for which many thanks.

At the castle I told the guard to help us up and I warned him. One word and I'd have his balls. They know Otto. Never say what I won't carry through.

Not for me to judge. I'd never have thought it. But then he's a man, isn't he, like the rest of us.

Got the fire going, mopped him up and put him to bed like a kiddie.

He muttered a few names. His wife's was one, I know that. His children's. And his horse.

I sat on for a bit in case he choked on his vomit. But he tossed a while and then he went off. I checked before I went down and his face was all smooth. Clear. He looked younger. Like people do when they're dead and those undertaker crows have done them up fancy.

Then, just as I was leaving I heard something and turned round. His eyes were open.

'Otto. I want you to do something for me. Between us. Try to find out about Antarah's sister. The missing girl. Manah.'

I woke once in the night from a dream of the pool at Tivoli. The old terror possessed me, of the immortal fish that can swallow the world, the weeds that snatch you down, to the fish which will eat your heart. The fear that death would be there where the spring bubbles and the fish dozes, and it would have my father's face.

But this time the panic slipped away and my mind was calmer than it had been. Otto had left the lamp and this, with the dying fire, made kind shapes of the shadows.

I thought of the pool and the desert and the oasis: the pool in the desert. There is beauty in both as well as horror. There may even be reconciliation.

I walked to the window, shakily, and looked out at the Valley of Tombs going away westward into night and remembered the thin curtain the Palmyrenes hung between life and death.

Are you there, Iamlichu, in those soft waves of sand, that inland sea of the spirit?

I drank water and went back to bed. My mind was clearer in other ways. I knew what I must do, my duty.

Winter is not yet here in full force. There are days of calm, bright weather. When the wind blows though, it is cold, from the north, and the men gathered in the agora shiver, though not altogether from the breeze.

The General and his officers stand on the platform of a ruined temple above the agora. Although he is shorter than Severus, Octavius remains a commanding figure.

The condemned have been tied to posts a few feet from the wall of the agora, and those who wish it, blindfolded. There are six of them. A couple are so weak they could not have stood without the posts. The firing party is ranged to attention about fifteen feet away. Otto, in his place on the steps that lead up to the platform, keeps his eye on the assembled men. He had a word with young Publius last night and is satisfied enough that there won't be any trouble from that direction. The boy's a professional, as his father was. He knows the rules.

The absolute silence is alarming. The shapes of everything in this clear light are strict, shadows unambiguous. A bird with ragged black wings coasts above the ruins and then, absurdly, a dog trots into that appalling silence, a yellowish desert dog. It will have been used to coming to the agora for leavings from the weekly Bedouin market. Otto is about to reach for a stone when the dog, having stood for a moment, puzzled, looks round, sniffs the air, whimpers and abruptly bolts as though it had, indeed, been stoned.

Procedure has been precisely observed. At the court-martial, Severus served for the defence, though with little hope. He had found it almost unendurable, talking to the prisoners. Their exhaustion and sickness was shocking but their seemingly passive acceptance of inevitable death was worse.

Finally, he brought himself to ask them why they came back. Bearing in mind the penalty for desertion, wouldn't it have been better to stay in the mountains and take their chance? He received no satisfactory answer. They seemed bewildered by his question.

Last night he himself took them food, wine, and beer, which they preferred, and sat with them. He urged them to write letters he would deliver to their families. He listened to those who wanted to talk. None spoke of the morning. Severus wondered: can they not imagine death? Perhaps not. If so, that was a mercy. He had never wished so profoundly that he had a faith, a consolation he might offer them.

At least, the General went against army orders in one respect. He refused to sentence them to crucifixion.

Everyone knows what is about to happen and yet it is a shock when the General raises his hand and the silence is cracked. There is something like a sigh from the men. The dead men slump, Zenobia's wall behind them.

The General steps forward.

'Let every man witness this,' he says, 'and know the penalty for desertion.'

Then he turns, his face blank as a stone, and leads the officers away, while Otto dismisses the men.

In his quarters, Severus throws olive-wood on the fire. He bends to reach for the diary under his mattress, but carefully, not to wake Ali. With his long lashes and delicate bones, the boy is most beautiful sleeping.

Severus smiles.

'Oh, Ali, if only I loved you, how simple it would be.'

At his small table, Severus opens the diary.

It's three weeks since the executions but I have to write this down.

I watched him closely throughout, partly because I couldn't bear to see what was going on. I'm sure I wasn't the only one to find the whole business repugnant. It was simply that I didn't trust myself to hide my squeamishness. Heaven knows how I'd get on if we ever see action. They say, after the first man you've killed, you feel sick and then you get over it. You're carried along with the rest. And if your own life depends on it, obviously you kill. I'm pretty sure I'd lose my scruples fast enough.

Through the whole ghoulish business, somehow the General seemed to be holding the rest of us at a distance. He watched everything that happened below in the agora until the surgeon had pronounced the men dead. I saw him – or, rather, I see him now – as taking the deserters' deaths upon himself, as though he were actually absorbing this necessary horror into his flesh, his bloodstream, his imagination, his will . . .

And what do I mean by that? I don't know. Although his face was blank there was something about him suggesting a heavy sorrow, despair.

We go into the desert in a few days, he and I. At least, I can do that for him. And my talk maybe entertains him a little.

As things get worse, my own optimism is under attack. But hopefulness is a strangely persistent instinct. Partly the pleasure of small things? Books. The scent and warmth of the fire. A new fleece I bought from Imru. Ali, who to please me paints his eyes with kohl, like a girl, and lets me oil his body and drench him in the rose-water of old Syria.

See them leave, taking the same route Octavius and Otto had followed earlier. Octavius and Severus on horseback. Jafnah rides a camel, leading another loaded with provisions and baggage. Dido disapproves, tossing her head, breaking into an uncomfortable jog-trot.

To preserve food for winter the whole camp, including the officers and the General, have been on short rations. Severus, always thin, shows the deprivation most but it is Octavius he worries about. There is something like a fever to the General, yet he shivers in the air of early morning.

The further they ride from the camp, the more desolate the landscape grows and the more it appears that Jafnah is the only one of the three at home in this terrain. The Bedouin can go all day without eating or drinking.

Under a thin sun the salt flats signal but the General does not turn his head. He has a heavy skull and over the years in Tadmor his short-cropped hair has grizzled.

Last night he said: 'Probus is right. This is a foolish and irresponsible adventure. You are free, Severus.'

* * *

He meant, to stay, not to accompany him. But how could I not go with him? If he rode into a ravine I'd follow.

I imagine sometimes his expression of bewilderment if I told him how I feel. It wouldn't be shock - simply puzzlement.

I wonder if he's heard any gossip about Ali. The boy was in tears last night, he held me as if he could stop me from leaving. Perhaps, after all, I'm not just a giver of presents? This morning he ran beside us, his hand on my stirrup. He reached up and I realised he had a present for me: a bracelet made of twisted camel-hair, with a red thread through it. No one noticed. I slipped it on. I'm wearing it now.

To the north and west of the city, mountains slip down like a falling wave to finger the site: Gebel Hayane, Gebel el Tarr and Gebel Mohammed ibn Ali.

But the party is riding east into a desert that appears at first to be a fearful place without features – except, of course, to Jafnah, for whom this is charted territory of tracks and wells and landmarks. He clicks his tongue and calls to his camel: yallah, get on. And then the other two see the outcrops of black basalt, formations of cooled lava, and they understand that this seeming nothingness was made by some extraordinary violence, the breaking of worlds.

And yet as the sun climbs, hotter than it has been lately, at the moment no more than pleasantly warm, and the horizon shivers into mirage, their spirits rise. Dido shifts to an easier trot. It is good to have left behind the garrison, to be riding even to an imaginary destination. There is an illusion of ordinary purpose, the pleasure of movement over the earth.

In the minds of Octavius and Severus Tadmor is diminished by distance, the further they travel east. So a vast plain becomes a cramped and confining place shouldered by mountains. Looking back they see it has gone along with the mountains, the quivering light and the horizon have swallowed them.

No one knows what Jafnah is thinking, and without Probus to translate conversation will be difficult. A little French, a little English, their few words of Arabic. He rides apart from them and slightly ahead.

For the moment there is no talk. All have pulled their kiffayahs across their mouths. Intimations of winter, and hunger, have laid most of the garrison low with some infection. Octavius still has the cough but as they pass the point he reached with Otto he feels almost carefree, pulls aside his headdress to call to Severus.

'This is better.'

There is a glitter about the General, perhaps from fever. He gives Dido her head and she breaks into a canter, he has to hold her from a gallop. She has never liked the company of camels, least of all to follow one.

Yes, Pausonias, I remember Herodotus. Cyrus defeated Croesus by mounting his cavalry on camels to frighten the horses. I liked that lesson.

But what are you doing on a mule? Too small for you, your wasted legs dangling absurdly below its barrelled ribs.

I thought we'd lost you long ago. You had gone off into eternity to argue with Gaius Germanicus: two old men in the sand disputing the universe and poetry and mathematics. I saw you beached in the Valley of Tombs.

'If I were doomed to eternity in this appalling place I would hope not to be in such company as that blinkered self-seeker.' Pausonias urges on his mule to catch up with Octavius. He had always been skinny but his bones now seem to shine through the thin covering of his flesh. 'So you remember Herodotus? He appealed to the young. Unreliable but entertaining.'

'I remember a desert tribe that never dreamed.'

Pausonias snorts.

'And dog-headed men. And winged snakes. And the

phoenix doubtless. Tell me, boy, is that what you are after? The Emperor hunts headless men with eyes in their breasts? The horned ass?'

'I think I'm looking for extinction. Or deliverance. I don't know which. I believe I am sick.'

In saying this, Octavius realises it to be true. In his mind destiny and destination have become blurred, the distinction between them lost. He has the idea that as they ride east their destiny is already forming. He has seen it as a lost palace or city. But it could also take on flesh and wear the blue-painted face of the Savage. Or it could be madness. Between here and the Euphrates he might become one of the tribe that never dream.

He is thinking how rarely in his life inclination has been allowed to overrule duty: normally they have been one and the same.

He feels Dido picking her way through a stretch of wicked black chips of stone. He hears the tinkle as the mule nearly slips. He lets Dido have the reins and senses that the mule is following where she steps.

In taking the same rations, often less than the men, Octavius may have held off mutiny.

But desertion? Desert. Deserter.

'You said once, Pausonias, that the desert and the sea are the same?'

'I'm seasick on this mule, if that is what you mean.'

Pausonias's voice is fading.

'I would never have taken you for a visionary, Octavius. You have many qualities but I did not realise that imagination was one of them.'

As he begins to tire a little, from hunger and fever, around the middle of the afternoon, the General loses the horizon and sees that the desert has liquidesced. It has turned to water, sometimes the green-black of the bottomless pool at Tivoli, sometimes the wide-eyed blue of the summer sea when he played on the beach at Ostia as a child.

Pausonias has left him but he rides happily now, his mind fixed on that beach, that child. He can smell the salt. He pokes with a stick at the small, anxious life in a rock-pool and for that afternoon the pool and the creatures within are all of his life.

Severus has been keeping an eye on the General. At one point this morning he seemed to be mumbling to himself.

Then, a mile or so after they have left behind the field of flints he sees that Octavius appears to have fallen asleep in the saddle. But then he is as at home on horseback as most men are in a chair.

With the weather less hot they carry on through the afternoon and then abruptly Jafnah grunts and gestures to them to stop.

The land looks as featureless as it has all day but Severus watches Jafnah with fascination as he dismounts and points to a shallow depression of stones, a thorn bush and more stones, heaped up into some kind of cairn. Then he nods, hobbles the camels and sets about unloading food and water skins, with three bed-rolls.

Severus slips from his horse and joins Octavius.

'How does he know to stop here?'

Octavius points.

'Those stones are a bed. The others probably a shelter against sandstorms. There was a well here but the Savages have poisoned it. So we carry our own water.'

The General hardly seems aware that he is coughing. Severus huddles by the fire, the fleece he bought from Imru around his shoulders. Otto had warned him: watch out for Jafnah, sir. I don't trust that bugger. Not that there is anything I could do if he chooses to cut our throats. On balance, I don't think he will. He has nothing to gain by our deaths. We're in an infernal place, with inadequate provisions and he knows he's the master here.

And yet, it's odd, in his way he still defers to the General. I think he's the only one of all of us Jafnah respects. There is some strange comradeship between them. It's beyond me.

Oh, Ali, I could do with the warm press of your body. I'm still wearing your bracelet. If the Savages get us I wonder what will become of you? Who'll give you presents then?

My love, this is such a beautiful night. Lying in this bed of stones hollowed out of the sand, I am unaccountably content. I know I'm sick, in the mind perhaps as well as the body, but I am glad to be where I am and were this trough to become the grave it resembles, the sands to cover me and fill my eyes and take my breath, I would regard that as a good end. I can even imagine that you and your Christians might be right, and I would wake into another life and find you beside me, in my arms.

When my mind is clear that is my problem. I cannot imagine a life everlasting of the spirit. When I think of you, you are the scent of your skin and hair, the touch of your cool hands, the warmth of your lips.

I saw Pausonias today. He hasn't changed. His flesh is almost gone but he was always a bag of bones.

I suppose I am nearly happy because it was a good evening, one in which I felt at home. To be free of the garrison, that was good, but it was better still to be a part of the life of a small desert camp. There was the groaning of camels in the night and the smell of them and of horses and a dung fire and camel's milk, which we drank with stale pitta bread, goat's curd and a handful of dates.

My fever keeps me warm even in this bitter night and by the fire I was alternately shivering and sweating.

Afterwards, Jafnah sat cross-legged by the fire, with his rifle to hand. At last he came out of his sulk, unable to resist the nomad's pleasure of talk at the end of the day. I think he and I have some kind of understanding.

I coughed and he jerked his head.

'I think you are sick.'

'It is not important.'

I have been struck before by the race-memory of the Bedouin. Hatim had talked to me of the ancient caliphs, the Ommayads, who loved the Bedouin and rode out from Damascus to pitch their tents in this desert, build their palaces and hunt with falcon for gazelle.

I asked Jafnah about them and he spoke, as though he were remembering his grandfathers, of Yezid, whose mother was Bedouin.

'He drank wine, and that made a fool of him. But a poet too.'

I asked him if he remembered any Arab poetry. Hatim had told me of some that were spoken on nights like this in ancient times. Many, he said, were of lost homes and camps, which in the telling, became evocations of a paradise to which there was no return.

Jafnah's face was blank. I thought he was bored again. He prodded the fire and as the sparks flew up so did his words, painfully translated.

'I have seen the fates stamp like a camel in the dark.'

This caught the attention of Severus. But I could see we'd get no more poetry from Jafnah.

Instead he looked at our map and jabbed a finger at tomorrow's route, which would take us away from the remains of the route to Dayr az Zawr, away from all landmarks recognisable to us.

Severus looked apprehensive but I was thankful to be going into this great nothingness.

The men think we are scouting for the Blue Warriors. And so we are. But Severus knows my true purpose and that it might be the death of us, yet he follows.

He must know that the General is mad, or nearly so. I can never return his faithfulness.

As we go on and abandon all sense, I feel sure, Livia, that I shall hear your voice and you mine. There is an extraordinary peace in the extremity to which I have taken us.

I think of you, and Rufus, and my father, wondering if I resemble him. Lying in this bed of stones I think that to go to bed at all is an imitation of death.

It would not be so bad to slip out of life now. In my ears there are the night-noises of a small camp, the smell of animals in the still air. While in my eyes there is a brilliant multitude of heavy stars.

But then, love, I feel you are close, you may even have joined us on this journey and I should try to live.

You know, Livia, don't you, I have always had difficulty living in the world of human passions. And now, just when I might die, I have such a yearning to find the way in: a door opening onto a brightly lit room.

Suddenly I'm so cold.

Jafnah is sitting guard. He has doused the fire to a small glow. I nodded goodnight and managed the few words of Arabic that mean, I think, may the morning find you well.

The General's eyes were open but he seemed not to see me. He was mumbling something I could not catch and shivering uncontrollably. I put my hand on his forehead. The fever has broken for the moment but this chill on his skin worries me almost as much.

He said something that sounded like his wife's name.

I covered him with Imru's fleece. Then I lay down beside him and held him in my arms to give him my warmth. At last he shook less and seemed to sleep.

How strange. The only bed I shall ever share with him is a hollow in the sand lined with stones.

17

My dear, I woke in the night to an absolute certainty that you are alive. I thought it might be a dream but in the morning I was still sure of it.

It was as if you had come to stand for a while by my bed. You've been in shadow for so long, your head turned away.

I was quite stupidly happy this morning and at the same time sharply afraid, as if I knew you were going into danger.

What is it, I wonder, between us? Love? Or a kind of tissue that grows in marriage through the years - so you sleep awkwardly, with your head on your hand, and in the morning my fingers are numb, I have to flex them and warm them.

Perhaps the two can be the same, the love and the habit of marriage?

In the milking hut before dawn, with the cow breathing down my neck and my face pressed against her flank, in the hay and milk warmth of cattle, my fingers unfroze and I was thinking of something I half remember from Homer, about the nobility of a long marriage. I talked to the cow and then sang. Not as silly as it sounds – talk and music calms them. She stopped trying to butt me or to kick over the bucket of blue milk. Can you imagine me as a milk-maid?

Going into the hut I had to break the icicles. It is winter at last up here and bitterly cold. But by the time I had finished and was carrying the bucket back to the kitchen the sun had come up and it was such a morning! Mist below and frost on the orchard.

Winter will be hard, I know, but there are compensations. We'll sit close to the fire, by the lamp, and sew and talk and spin and weave.

I didn't tell you, did I, that I've penetrated the deep mystery of spinning and weaving? So I can turn a fleece into a rug, a bedcover or a piece of knitting.

We talk less and less about our former lives. Perhaps to stay sane we have to live in the present. So only in the tales we tell the children to put them to sleep do we speak of the past, weaving it as we talk into a story of a place faraway, as distant as another country.

I wonder if we are preparing them for permanent exile or for possible return? Now and then we do talk of going back but we hear from Jerome that the new Christianity has nothing to do with the old church I once loved. It is a hysterical and vengeful faith, one that Christ would have abhorred. Poor Jerome finds himself the puppet of a theocracy as savage as the brief regime of Lucius Tarquinius.

I'm weary, love, that's the truth. If I were alone and responsible only to myself, I might go back to Tivoli and take my chance. But I look at Paulina and see you and Rufus.

It is such an astonishing blessing to know that you are alive. But I sense too that you are on some journey of great peril – whether of the mind or the body, I can't tell.

I wish I could ride with you. Perhaps I shall.

18

In the night there had been a light snowfall. There were a few melting flakes on Imru's fleece.

There seems no hope of sun today and yet the journey continues towards a destination in which Severus has almost ceased to believe.

At dawn they make a small breakfast of flaps of pitta bread and water. The General seems to have difficulty swallowing. He is still coughing. His face has thinned and there are dark smudges under his eyes but when asked if he slept well, he nods. His voice is hoarse. Severus has the impression that he is eating and drinking only to forestall questions.

'We leave the map today, Severus.'

'Sir.'

There is the business of breaking camp. Watering and feeding the horses. The camels have grazed on plants so small and sickly it seems impossible they could provide nourishment. Complaining, all the beasts are reluctant to get moving, as if they smelled danger, snuffed it up, were somehow aware of the folly of the expedition.

'How long?' Severus asks Jafnah, who holds up his forefinger: one day.

Jafnah covers the remains of the fire with sand, scans the earth and removes all traces of their stay, burying even the dung of the animals.

As they ride off, leaving the track behind them, into a scree that is part broken stones, part sand, featureless to all but Jafnah, Severus almost laughs at the odd company they make: one purblind, leading, another probably mad and certainly sick, himself as helpless as a child, following for reasons he has forgotten, and because he could never find the way back.

They talk very little. There is the dip and sway of the camels. They have a rolling movement, like sailors ashore. Jafnah rides in the Arab way, both feet on the same side, one ankle resting on the other. Dido side-steps if the camels come too close. In the grey light that contains the little company Octavius, ahead of Severus, his cloak falling over Dido's rump, presents a shape that is neither horse nor man, as though he had ridden into mythic territory.

A slight breeze comes up. It brings not air but sand and a souring and thickening of the atmosphere, so for a moment Severus loses sight of Octavius. This ominous desert challenges and blurs all ordinary concepts of reality.

When he catches him up Severus notices that the General is riding, his gaze ahead, as if he knows the path.

'Did you know, Severus, the Roman Christians believed barbarians to be instruments of divine punishment.'

At the thought of the Blue Warriors Severus shivers.

'I'm wondering if we're lost, sir.'

But the temporary clear-headedness has gone. As the day advances the General can no longer distinguish between the living and the dead. He mumbles and coughs. Once he calls Severus Rufus.

Another time he says, 'Pausonias here is of the opinion that we were wrong to forget history. So we are enduring it again.'

Some time in the afternoon Livia joins them. Octavius has been expecting her. She rides a pony and her head is uncovered.

'You see, my love, my hair has turned white.'

'It's still beautiful.'

'Yours, too,' she says fondly. 'And you are so thin.'

'Will you ride with us a while?'

'As long as I can.'

She sits well on her pony, her back straight. Her white hair, thick, is caught at the nape of the neck with a tortoiseshell clip. A thick grey shawl is over her shoulders and tied in front.

Quite suddenly, in this muddy light, they come across ruins of an Ommayad pleasure-castle. A turret. And then a broken archway half buried in the earth. Octavius and Livia rein in their horses for a moment, to listen to the music of the lute and the Arab viol, the night talk and laughter. In their eyes there are companionable fires and these miniature palaces with their frescoes of plump dancing-girls, forbidden by Allah, rise again and are triumphantly restored.

And then the wind drops and snow and sleet put out those summer fires.

Severus says to Jafnah: 'The General is no longer responsible. We must turn back.'

Jafnah clicks his tongue.

'We are soon there.'

Severus pulls the scarf across his mouth. There is grit in the dashing sleet. In this yellowing air you could hallucinate as with a summer mirage. For a second he thinks he can see another figure riding beside the General.

In the late afternoon Severus wakes, not knowing he had fallen asleep in the saddle.

Jafnah shouts. He holds up his hand. Severus reaches for his rifle but the shape so alarmingly forming is inanimate. At first it looks like the black fin of a shark. Then it is gone. Then it is the jagged wing and carcass of an aircraft.

Jafnah slides from his camel. They have arrived. Of the body of the plane only the ribs remain, scorched and twisted.

Severus dismounts and blinks the sleet from his eyes. He

and Jafnah stay back as Octavius approaches the wreck.

He stands bare-headed in the falling snow, the snow settling on his shoulders, then melting.

The plane might have been pecked clean – nothing is left but the bare metal bones.

'The pilot?' Severus wonders.

'Blue Warriors,' Jafnah says. He spits against the evil eye.

'He must have been dead when he crashed. What would they want with a dead body?'

Jafnah shrugs. It could be anywhere. Then he grins and points at his yellow teeth.

Cannibals?

Severus thinks, I am the one who is mad, to follow him.

There is something else about the wreck now he comes to look closer. He approaches the General and points out faded rags tied to the superstructure. And there are other small mysteries: a string of beads, another of gilt coins and a cracked clay bowl.

'What does it mean?'

At first he thinks the General has not heard him. But then he answers.

'This is a holy spot, a shrine. Those are tokens of worship.' He turns and looks at Severus as though recognising him. 'I had no right to bring you here. It is terrible.'

Severus steps back a few paces. As the snow parts for a moment, he sees what Octavius sees: a long spear planted in what would have been the cockpit bears a skull, which has in turn been crowned with a circlet of twisted wire and more rags.

Octavius falls to his knees, Dido, a white horse in a white scene, snorting and nuzzling his shoulder.

'This is the place,' he says.

They huddle by Jafnah's fire in the shelter of the wreck or the church or the memorial, or whatever it is. Now the snow has begun to fall in earnest the air is warmer than on most desert nights.

Unseen by both Severus and Jafnah, Livia is there too. Pausonias and Gaius Germanicus play chess by the light of the fire and by some inner light bestowed upon them by death.

Octavius fainted after he knelt but now he is conscious again, coughing, stretched on a prayer-mat beneath Imru's fleece. He is fascinated to watch the game. Gaius Germanicus plays rationally and mathematically but Pausonias has the cunning.

Octavius sees the whole game, complete, finished. Pausonias will win. Octavius smiles, shuts his eyes and sleeps. He wakes to find Severus bending over him.

'Sir, will you take some food?'

'My wife was here but she has gone, I think.'

'Jafnah says we must leave at dawn.'

The General drinks a little, Severus supporting him. He seems to recognise the lieutenant for the first time in many hours.

'How strange, Severus. I had thought it would be a palace. An oasis like Tadmor. Jafnah knew.'

'Perhaps he tricked us.'

'Perhaps. He never said it would be a palace. But it would be a good joke.' The General licked his dry lips. 'To teach us that there is no earthly paradise. Nor does salvation fall like snow.'

The General's voice is faint. Severus kneels to listen.

He says: 'But to worship that horrible thing.'

'A man. Invested with the divine. As we all are. We are our own priests. We must forgive ourselves. To be human. If I live until first light, help me up, Severus. If not, there must be no mourning.'

His eyes close. His sleep this time is quiet, so still that Severus bends closer to feel the General's breath on his own cheek.

* * *

It takes Jafnah and Severus together to get Octavius mounted, more or less, on Dido. His grip on the reins is weak and he sways in the saddle but he appears to understand.

As they start out on the long journey the snow still falls, though not to settle.

With difficulty Octavius looks back once. He sees whatever he sees. Severus follows his gaze. There is the fin of the plane, receding, and it could be a trick of the uncertain light on the retina, but it appears to the lieutenant that attenuated blue figures have grouped themselves around the shrine. They are unnaturally tall or else they are riders. He is about to call to Jafnah, then he turns once more, and the Savages are gone: creatures of sand or snow, simulacra of men.

Most of the time Octavius allows Dido to carry him. Sometimes he follows Livia's pony. She pauses to allow him to catch up.

'Rufus is dead, my darling. We must bear it.'

'Yes.'

The General has fallen asleep or fainted in the saddle, but Dido carries him so kindly. The small caravan stops for nothing. In the afternoon the wind comes up from the east, the warmer quarter. The sky clears and as they ride across the sea of ancient lava and stone and sand, they glimpse, even before Tadmor, the glittering peaks of the Anti-Lebanon.

The camels are far ahead. Smelling home, Dido trots faster. Then, like a mirage, the stones of Tadmor seem to rush together, building the city.

19

In my sickness Hatim came to me once. My old friend sat for a while by my couch. I always enjoyed our silences.

Finally he said: 'So you have had your vision?'

My tongue was too thick to speak and I was alternately burning up in the desert, entering the heart of the fire itself, and then the breath struck by cold from my body in the depths of Tivoli's icy pool. I saw Rufus there, swimming with the immortal fish, and I woke in tears. I saw Hatim leave, pausing at the door to raise his hand in salute, his wand-like figure wavering in the firelight.

I thought I recognised someone else: Otto, his face creased with concern. And was that Severus standing beside him?

Someone was sponging my face.

I was on a journey all that time, often exhausted by the voyage but not afraid, whatever the outcome. I stood sometimes at the corner of the room and saw myself, the patient on the couch, those who came and went, and I wanted to console them, to say: that is nothing, a husk.

Ali, I still wear your bracelet. I touch it now. At night I forget sometimes and wake expecting to find you curled on the mat beside my bed. My body remembers yours but what use is that?

I was so exhausted by the journey and the weather and my anxiety for the General, I didn't realise for a moment that the Bedouin camp was smaller. I could see Antarah's tent but not Imru's.

And then inside the garrison, past the watch-tower, there was a peculiar silence. Otto was calling for help to get the General to his quarters. I went to mine where food had been set out and wine. The fire had been lit. I planned to eat and drink and then to bathe in the hot spring. I must have fallen asleep because I woke to find Probus was standing by the fire, looking solemn.

Poor Probus. He would find it hard even to imagine that there might be more to homosexuality than the physical mechanics, to him so repellent. And he'd be the first to admit that imagination is not his strong suit.

I smiled and offered him wine. He shook his head. And then he told me, Ali, that your body had been found, butchered, on the sacrificial stone in the Temple of Bel. A sacrifice to Al-Uzza, Venus, the evening star. Antarah had explained to him. He was ashamed for his own people. Those who had fled were the perpetrators.

I said stupidly: 'I heard they had gone back to the old faiths.'

He nodded. 'Hardship, winter and fear of the Savages. I'm sorry. We found this.'

He gave me the handkerchief with my initial, my present to you so horribly returned. Your blood on it.

'They buried him in the Valley of Tombs.'

'Yes.'

Before he left he said once more: 'I'm sorry.'

I think then I drank without getting drunk but enough to put me to sleep for a short time, because I woke shivering, still in my wet clothes, imagining I'd had a bad dream, to find the fire dead and the wine spilled on the couch and on the handkerchief, your blood and that red wine.

Pissing rain. Snow was bad enough but this is worse. Gets in your head.

Not like Otto to be as down as this but I reckon this is the worst winter since we came. Not just the weather. That wanker lieutenant with the pretty face says he saw the Savages out there. Then while they were having their tea-party in the desert the Bedouin are screaming and shouting in the night. Probus says leave them to it, and what could we have done? We're half-starved and they're off their heads. But none of us expected what happened. That boy. Otto knew what went on with Severus but the lad didn't deserve that.

Savages, all of us, I suppose, in one way or another. I've been a regular long enough to tell you a thing or two about what men are capable of.

And with the General still sick, it's like the earthquake again. You don't know where you are.

So Imru and his lot are gone and good riddance and you can see something's boiling up between Antarah and that one-eyed camel-jockey, Jafnah.

I got Probus to ask Antarah about his sister, that Bedouin girl the General talks about, the one he's known since she was a kiddie. Manah. When she was hardly grown she was flaunting it about, I'd say, asking for it, and I'd have given it to her myself if she'd looked twice at me. Out of bounds or not.

So Antarah looks grim and says she's disgraced his people. Probus reckons he doesn't know where she is. He says those Moslems sometimes stone a woman to death or strangle her. I don't see Antarah himself doing that. Imru maybe. But Antarah's got more of the old chief in him, Hatim. As gypsies go, he wasn't so bad.

What I reckon is, we might make it to the spring and then it'il be the end of us, one way or another.

Sooner maybe for the General. Queer how calm he seems. Now and then I could swear he recognised me. Once he looked straight at me and smiled and said my name: Otto.

* * *

Darling,
I must tell you first that Rufus is dead. He survived the African campaign and was back in Tivoli. Then there was a swimming accident. He drowned in that pool where you all used to bathe, where we first met. You remember the first time that nearly happened?

I can only put it like this, baldly and plainly. I believe that we'll have the chance to grieve together. I can't write more about it here, or my feelings. How terrible that this is the first letter I have written in years that there is a chance of you reading.

It seems he acquitted himself well. He was promoted. A good soldier. A popular boy, I was going to say, but, of course, he was a man.

When I heard about Rufus I fell ill. Some kind of fever. I'm better now but my mind is so confused. Anne, who looked after me, made herbal infusions, coaxed me to eat and get up, says that at the height of my delirium I seemed to be dreaming of you, or, rather, talking to you. She says at one point I called out. And I started raving about snow in the desert, as if there could be such a thing!

Now I'm sitting by the fire too weak even to knit but much better, well enough for them to tell me the news, good and bad.

Jerome, that gentle man, was crucified in Tivoli on St Stephen's day. There, I have said it.

This terrible act was a miscalculation that set the people in revolt. The military have taken over and if this peace holds we may even be able to return! But so many gone and so little left of our beloved Tivoli. How our great world has shrunk, armies on all frontiers recalled. We shall be like a small household that has retreated, exhausted, within its walls, thankful if we are left alone to tend our gardens.

How strange, that's what I used to dream of. Tired soldiers coming home to their vineyards. But the other part of my dream will not come true. The dead on the distant battlefields will not awake. We shall never see Rufus again.

It's February. The snow has melted for the moment and today I took a few steps outside. I could hear the slap of snow falling from the trees and the stream boiling over its banks. There were a few green shoots. The lambing on the lower pasture has started already.

And now I must send this letter. The convoy from Tivoli has rested the night here and is on its way south-east.

I hardly know myself in the mirror. My hair has turned quite white.

Goodnight, my love.

Livia.

I came to my full senses the day the convoy from Tivoli arrived. Half a dozen exhausted men.

At least, I was able to stand and meet them, dressed in the rags of a General, Severus and Probus beside me. I saw the shock in their faces at our appearance; before they could check themselves their eyes mirrored our condition: gaunt and tattered.

We had seen them coming from a long way. This was the end of February and the sky had cleared. The guard made out the figures, insects creeping down the mountainside. We feared Savages.

I ordered a feast. Otto plundered what is left of our stores. Probus went to bargain with Antarah and came back with a goat, a little maize and some milk and unleavened bread. We brought out the last of our wine. There was a precious letter from Livia which I saved to read when I was alone.

Four were army commanders, two senators, one of whom, Sabinus, I knew as a boy when he too was a pupil of Pausonias's. They reported on the state of affairs in Tivoli, the horrors of Lucius Tarquinius's reign and the theocracy that followed.

We spoke little and when we did our voices sounded to us rusty in our throats. The three of us, Severus, Probus and myself , looked more like savages than army officers.

Probus is not the greatest talker at the best of times. Severus did his best. He has not lost his grace and humour but his youth has gone. I look back on our early days, among the ruins, in the hot-spring baths; I remember how he named the stars for me, our talks about poetry and history, and those times seem as far away as childhood. Further, perhaps, for I've come to realise how the child in us can never be put aside by experience; we look out still upon the world with dazzled eyes. Is that what Livia meant when she teased me for my innocence? An inappropriate quality, I suppose, to find in a grizzled veteran. But then I have been mad.

These thoughts were going through my head as they talked around my table. I was dizzy. I should have refused wine.

I said: 'We took you at first for Savages.'

They told us that the story among the few people they met was that the Blue Warriors had been in the hills but vanished in the first snow-storm. There were rumours that they held the passes into Syria from Lebanon, that they had sacked Baalbek. The only certain thing seems to be that they have stopped short at the Mediterranean.

They said that among many others, a sect has surfaced at home of fanatics who believe we should welcome the Savages as warriors of god. They urge soldiers to lay down their arms and join them. They await the coming of a barbarian messiah from the desert.

Sabinus stayed on by my hearth when the others had left.

'Strange times,' I said. 'You remember? Pausonias used to advise us to avoid history.'

Sabinus smiled. 'Yes, I remember. You were his favourite pupil, you know.'

'I can't believe that.'

Sabinus told me some of the news I read later in Livia's letter. Not all of it. Of course, I said nothing of the journey in the desert and those I had met there. I mentioned the terrible death of the Bedouin boy, Ali, but not the connection with Severus.

I'd realised long ago about Severus but it seemed of no importance. Watching him now, guessing that he feels guilty about the boy, I remember Pausonias's servant and lover coming to me so long ago with the inscribed copy of Plato, just after his master's death.

Sabinus said: 'We'll have to wait out the winter with you. Next month the mountains should be clear of snow.'

I nodded. For a while we sat in silence, both drowsy from the wine and exhaustion. We heard a shout from the barracks. I had told the men that afternoon that they would be going home. Later I must prepare them for what we may find at Tivoli. Many will have lost families and homes.

I yawned. 'So Empires fall. As Pausonias would say. With satisfaction.'

Sabinus was very quiet and then I realised he was watching me with a strange expression.

'Would it surprise you to know that you have become a kind of god at home? The people remember you. You could come back as a divine Emperor, Augustus. You have not been tainted. And you would have the support of the Military Command.'

I refused, of course, and Sabinus did not press the matter. I did not tell him that I had seen a god in the desert, that skull crowned with twisted wire and rags, the wind blowing through it.

I shivered. The fire was almost out. I touched Livia's letter in my pocket.

If Sabinus had known in what a strange world I lived, between the living and the dead, the spirits crowding at my back as vivid as he seemed to himself in his own mirror.

In my sickness I had dreamed what Livia had to tell me. All

the same I dismissed Otto and sat out that night.

Old Hatim came to me for the last time. He was sitting in Sabinus's place on the other side of the hearth.

He said: 'It is a terrible thing to lose a son. You must take this too, into your flesh.'

He kept me company all that night. And then he clicked his tongue and was gone, raising his hand in farewell, just as he had when I saw him riding between the lights of the guard-posts, beyond the palm grove into the desert. And then the shades of that queer country received him.

20

We found Manah in March in the hypogeum Severus and I had discovered all those years ago. Her body was hooped around a bundle of rags, the stillborn child of my frenzy when the earthquake seemed the forerunner of the breaking of worlds.

Before her own death Manah had tried to bite through the cord. Severus found her first. Privately, he gave me the tin imperial eagle she had clutched in her hand, a present I had once given to a girl playing by the stream, who made me think of my own children.

Unlike the others, this was a death I could never forgive myself nor speak of, so I must live unshriven. Perhaps this is the human condition.

Cast out by her own people, she must have scavenged somehow to live long enough to give birth. I ordered her body to be taken to Antarah for burial. If he understood, he said nothing. The dead child was a boy and I tried to see that pathetic corpse as my second son. I thought, I should name it but I could not. Rufus was then too present to me.

Severus helped me to heave the stone back into place.

I feel faint, my eyelids forced painfully open in the sly brilliance of advancing spring.

Spring slops down the mountains as melting snow.

After a day and a night of rain from the Mediterranean the wadis become rivers and I ride out with Severus. Grass veils the slopes and there is a carpet of sweet-smelling flowers. However often we have seen this miracle it still surprises us, this boiling into life of dead land.

Severus slips from his horse and kneels to look at something. Then he shows me.

'Have you ever seen a desert rose?'

It is beautiful but not a flower at all. A perfect crystalline rose. Severus explains how water rises from the earth leaving salts. He gives it to me. I shall save it for Livia.

Bedouin women are driving their flocks to graze. Jafnah left yesterday with his people. I had paid him the rest of the gold. He had not betrayed me. He came to take his leave and I looked into his clouded eyes and asked him why?

'You say your wells are poisoned. The Savages are to the East. We have seen them.'

He gave that characteristic jerk of the head, impatient and mocking.

'Let my nephew be the farmer. He will grow fat and pick dates. One day he will build himself a house like you, General. He will be a woman who keeps chickens.'

Then he called to his camel: hut hut. I watched the caravan ride off until they were no more than a scribble in the sand. Antarah would be thankful, I thought. He grows more like Hatim every day, I can see my old friend's soul in him. I fear for him and his people when the Savages come.

At our backs the garrison is preparing for the journey. Probus and Otto are supervising. To cross the mountains we shall take only what we can carry ourselves or pack on mules and horses.

It is strange but I cannot imagine going home or what home will be, except for Livia. Nor can Severus, I know.

He says: 'Sabinus tells me you have been deified.'

I laugh. 'A tired old god.'

He hesitates. 'In the desert? That thing?'

'I saw something, Severus, or I thought I did. God or man. God in man.'

We sit for a while. My neck aches, reminding me of the wound in Africa. I think how through my many years of service I have come to see the map unmade, countries and frontiers lost. How would the chart remake itself? Where, secretly, obscurely, is some new empire beginning to form itself? Somewhere in the wake of the Savages is there a tribe, burying its dead, washing the sand from its eyes in the river, looking up, dreaming already of new lands?

The warm air that shows us up, deathly pale, has made the horses frisky. We race back to the garrison.

I try to prepare the men for what they may find if we make it home but they don't believe me. Their home fires, their families, their fields and streets have remained intact in their tired minds. Neither their wives nor their children nor their parents have aged or changed or died.

At this extreme of our lives in Tadmor this is all that sustains them. They have made a heaven of home, where their desert sores will be healed, the weariness slip from their limbs, their hunger be fed. And they will breathe sweet air and sleep with their women and their vines will flourish.

This morning I gave a last order, for that terrible cross to be burned. In spite of the recent rain it went back quickly to the ashes of carbon from which it had first been formed, the same from which we all sprang and to which we shall return. I accept this now: our inevitable mingling with the matter of the universe.

This last evening I walk alone in the Valley of Tombs.

Kithoth, Iamlichu, Banai, Laascha, Arraum, Hairan, Sabeis, Elascha, Bolma, Elahbel, Saquai, Moqimo, Maani, Athenathau, Atenatan, Hairan, Bolha, Breiki.

Those are the names of the wistful dead who whispered to me so long ago. To them I add: Rufus, Hatim, Manah, and the dead boy whose blood still stains the altar-stone.

They call to me once more and snatch at my tattered cloak, begging, tempting. They crowd me and, for the dead, their breath is sweet. It would be so easy to walk on.

But I turn away from the setting sun, back along the stone path that leads to the city where the evening tide of gold washes the ruins, and to whatever remains of my life.

At my back eternity sighs and for the moment folds her violet wings.

The author acknowledges W. G. Shepherd's translation of Horace's *The Complete Odes and Epodes*, Penguin Classics.

Thanks for their help to Donald Foster and Souhil Daas.